Give it to Me

ML NYSTROM

HOT TREE PUBLISHING

For information, contact the publisher, Hot Tree Publishing.

www.hottreepublishing.com

Editing: Hot Tree Editing

Cover Designer: BookSmith Design

Ebook ISBN: 978-1-922359-69-8

Paperback ISBN: 978-1-922359-70-4

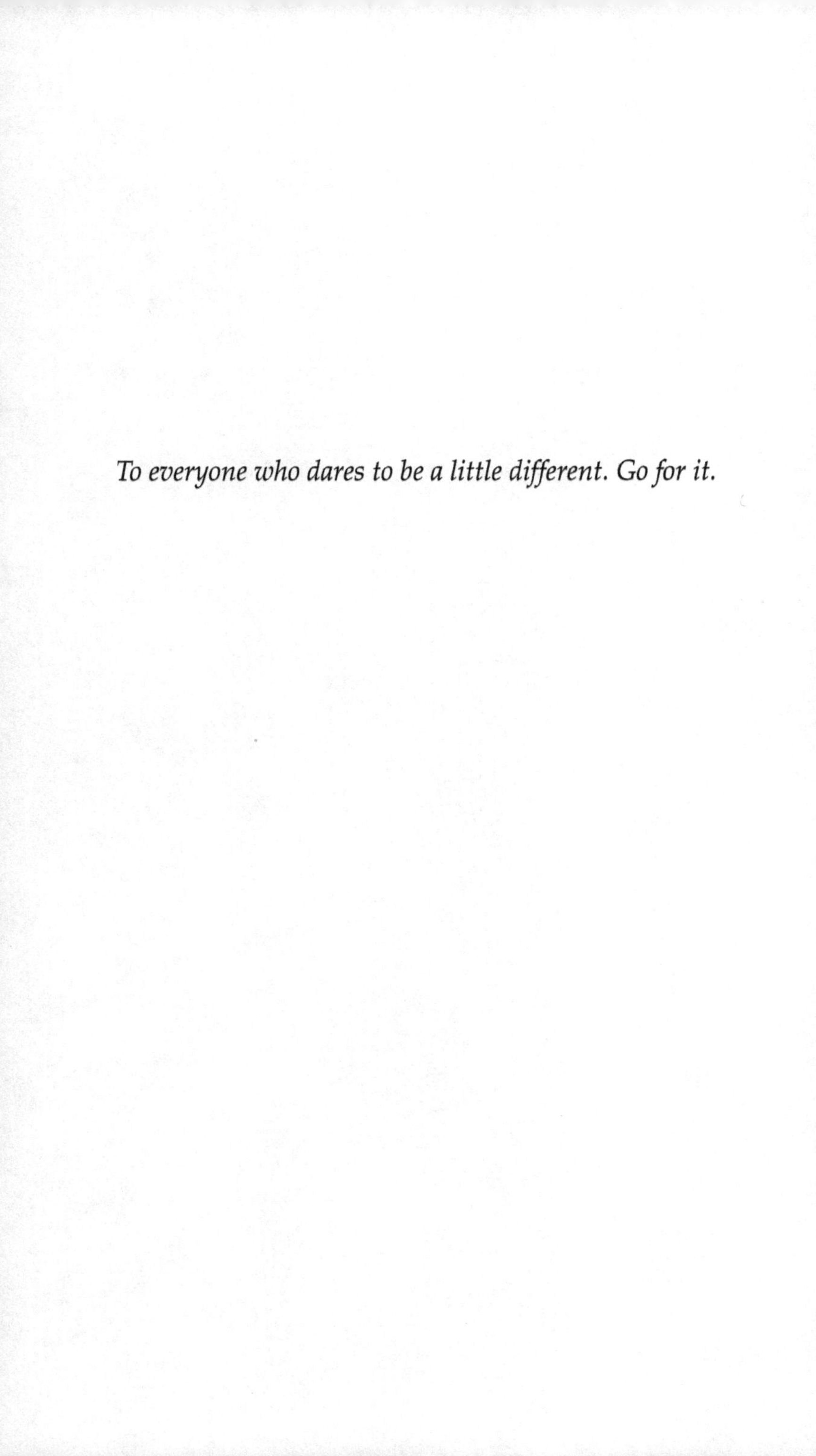

To everyone who dares to be a little different. Go for it.

PROLOGUE

"Oh my God, we're gonna get in so much trouble!"

Lana shot me a disgusted look. "We won't if you stop acting like a kid."

"We are kids. *High school* kids."

"We're eighteen already and almost graduated. Quit bitching." She stopped at the dark street corner and peered at the sign. "I think this is it."

I twisted my fingers together. My best friend, Lana, convinced me to sneak out of the hotel with her tonight and go exploring. Our school volleyball team made the nationals, and we'd traveled to Atlanta to compete all weekend. Unfortunately, we got knocked out in the second round and would head home tomorrow. Since it was our last night in this huge city, Lana decided we needed to go find some fun.

I wanted to find a fancy coffee and donut shop. She wanted to find something else.

Somehow she got a hold of a couple of tickets to a special midnight adult show at a private club, and she was determined to go.

"I bet there'll be at least some male strippers, Rhyleigh. When was the last time you saw a nice fat dick?"

I didn't want to admit I'd never seen one in person. Just the ones she showed me in the hidden porn collection she'd found in her brother's room. He had a box under his bed filled with pictures of men and women having sex in weird twisted positions. The faces of the people were supposed to show the throes of ecstasy, but some of them looked painful and strange.

"Where did you get those things, anyway?"

"Some old guy at the bar left them on his table. I swiped them when he wasn't looking."

"How do you know it's a male strip show?"

She pointed to the ticket. "See? Says *Master Johnson*. You know what a Johnson is, right?"

We left the city train station and walked three blocks to the address on the tickets. The dark building looked a little like an old hotel, but all the windows were blacked out. The guy at the front didn't ask for IDs when we approached the front door. He simply took the tickets and let us in.

Heat flushed my face as we entered the building. "Oh my God, please don't let us get kidnapped and sent to be sex slaves in Outer Mongolia."

"Rhyleigh, shut up!"

I shut it. People filled the room that looked like a theater foyer. The attire ran from cocktail dresses to jeans to black leather and studs. There were more men than women, and a number of people wore masks. I squeaked as a waitress walked by us with a tray full of champagne flutes. She wore an elaborate feathered mask and black thong, but nothing else. Her high breasts bounced with every step her stilettos took on the carpet. One of her nipples had a gold hoop piercing. I tried not to stare at it or her, but Lana pointed it out to me with her usual degree of discretion.

"Look at that. Ooh, I bet that hurt."

The woman stopped and held the tray out to us. "Not too much. It was worse when I got my hood done."

"Your hood?" The question came out of my mouth before I could stop it.

Her sculpted eyebrows came together in a frown. "Are you old enough to be here?"

My heart pounded hard enough I thought it

would burst from my chest. *Oh my God, we're going to jail!*

Lana took a glass and scoffed at me. "Stop being a dumbass. You know what a hood piercing is." She turned to the quizzical waitress to explain, "This is her first time to one of these and she's nervous."

I wasn't sure the woman bought Lana's answer, but she smiled and nodded as she addressed me directly. "Don't worry about what you'll see. It's a little shocking the first time, but really beautiful. Master Johnson is one of the best riggers around, and his wife's been his bottom for years. Everything is consensual and safe. We'll be loading in a few minutes, so enjoy the show."

She left, and I quietly hissed at Lana, "This is your first time too. So what is a hood piercing?"

She lifted one shoulder and grimaced at the taste of the champagne. "Blech, this is nasty. No, I don't know what it is, but Google has the answers. We'll look it up when we get back to the hotel."

My anxiety shot high when the red doors to the stage opened. We entered a theater in-the-round and found our seats. I looked around nervously at the scaffolding on the stage. Hooks and pulleys hung down from the sturdy framework, and a neat pile of multicolored coiled ropes sat in one corner.

"You sure this is a stripper show?"

Lana eyed the odd-looking setup, and for the first time, lost her bluster. "Um… maybe not?"

"We should go."

"We'd have to climb over a bunch of strangers to get to an exit. That would draw too much attention to us and guarantee we'd get in trouble. Let's just watch what happens. That waitress said it's really beautiful once you get over the first look."

"Like a hood piercing?"

"Shut *up*, Rhyleigh."

The house lights dimmed, and I held my breath. A blue spotlight came up slowly on a woman standing on the stage. Her straight hair shimmered in the light, and she wore a simple white robe. A smattering of applause sounded through the theater, and both Lana and I followed suit. A man in a Japanese kimono came up behind the woman as soft ethereal music started playing. He plucked at the robe, lifting it away from the woman's shoulders. She was naked underneath. It was clear from her body she was not young. Her breasts lacked the perkiness of youth and her stomach protruded with softness. Her demeanor said she didn't care. Her head lifted high as the cloth slipped down her body and a gentle smile appeared on her face. She didn't try to cower or cover herself from the audience. Instead, she radiated pride in her appearance. I found myself enthralled and a little jealous of her confidence.

The man plaited her hair in one long braid and folded it under itself to secure the strands. The whole time the woman stood still, resembling a nude marble statue like the kind in an art museum. He took great care not to pull or jerk and stroked her like he would a favorite beloved pet while he tended to her. His fingers trailed her cheek, and she leaned into his touch, her smile still soft. My stomach bloomed with unfamiliar heat at the tenderness and love between them. I'd never seen the kind of connection they had in anyone else. Not my parents or their country club friends. Not the couples that got together at school. Not even in movies. The depth between the two people on that stage was something so profound, my eyes teared up at its splendor.

"Well shit, I thought we'd see some cute, young dicks waving around, not some old-married couple. This is boring."

"We're stuck. You said so yourself. Now hush before someone sics an usher on us."

Lana crossed her arms and sat back in a snit. I turned my attention back to the stage.

The man picked up one of the red coiled ropes, and the blue light made it look neon purple. He started wrapping it around the woman's arms, binding them behind her back in an elaborate criss-cross shape. More coils went around her stomach and thighs. The entire process took several minutes while the music kept playing. The lights faded from blue to pink to gold to green to red. Over and over.

I watched the woman's face while her husband wound rope after rope until she couldn't move. Her legs were covered in diamond-shaped knots, but it was her face that intrigued me the most. Ecstasy, pure ecstasy shone from her as she was tied up. He touched her with gentle hands, controlling her body with the intricate design. She let him bend her arms and legs however he wanted, binding and constricting her movements until she had no control over herself. They looked like they didn't care that there were several hundred eyes watching this intimate moment. Their world only occupied the two of them.

He draped several more ropes from the scaffolding and attached them to her shoulders, waist, hips, knees and ankles, until she looked like she was caught in a spider's web. Once done, he stepped behind her and lifted his hands to cup and hold her breasts. Her head fell back, and he kissed her neck.

A moan in front of me caught my attention. A woman had her breasts out, and the man next to her had his mouth all over them. Another woman further down looked like she had her legs spread with her hands in between her thighs.

I swallowed the squeak in my throat and snapped my eyes back to the stage. The man moved back from the woman and asked her something. She nodded. With one huge pull, all the draped ropes lifted the woman in the air, arching her back and drawing her legs apart. The crowd shared a gasp at the move and applauded. Master Johnson approached the dangling woman and made some adjustments. He spun her in a long, slow circle, displaying his work to the appreciative audience. When he stopped her spin, he pulled some ropes and released others, putting the woman in a new shape before spinning her again. Upside down in a fetal position, on her side with her legs bent back, facing down, legs curled underneath, spin after spin after spin.

I tried not to glance at the other audience members, but it was hard to keep my eyes to myself. Muted sighs, whimpers, oohs, and ahhs surrounded me. The mysterious spot between my legs pulsed and grew heavy. Heat rose in me and the urge to squirm in my seat intensified. Even though I was one of the few virgins left in the school, I wasn't stupid. Plenty of sex talk happened in the locker room during gym class and team meets. I knew what a clitoris was and how it worked. I just hadn't explored mine yet. Locker room talk indicated that girls who masturbated were no more than horny sluts who couldn't keep a boyfriend. I wasn't sure I agreed, especially as at the moment, I wanted to touch myself so badly, I ached with the need.

Master Johnson slowly spun his wife so her open legs straddled his hips. She was secured in a horizontal position to the floor, carefully tied in a web of colored ropes. He pulled one suspended strand and her knees pulled back, further opening her core to him. He untied the belt to his kimono and let it slip from his body. His ramrod dick stood straight out from a bushy ball sack.

I held my breath, gaze intent, mesmerized as he cupped himself and fitted his hard dick between the woman's legs. She cried out as he pushed into her with one hard thrust.

Half the audience cried with her.

My mouth watered, and I swallowed several times to clear it. The man pounded into his wife and she writhed against the restrictive ropes. He used the suspension to drive inside her, swinging her body into his. I watched as he licked his thumb and put it between her legs. Another cry came from her, this time a long keening one of satisfaction. The man rammed in her one last time and roared his own release.

I shook lightly, my head buzzing and body pulsing with a need I didn't exactly understand. Shame and guilt rose up in me, and I bit my lip to keep tears from forming in my eyes. I didn't know why I felt this way, and I wanted to run. Escape from this place and never look back.

Confusion raced through me, not understanding my reaction. I liked what I saw, a lot. The knowledge sent a bolt of fear through me.

The moments then passed in a haze: the applause, the shuffling from the room, the journey to the train station.

Once on the train, Lana complained all the way back to the hotel. "Nasty. Who wants to watch two old people fucking? Gross! What a fucking waste of time."

I made humming noises to agree with her and make her happy, but my head drifted to relive the ending scene. Master Johnson untied his wife with as much care as he had when he started. He kissed the marks on each part of her skin as he revealed the expanse of milky white flesh. Worshipful. Reverent. Adoring. His last act was to place the robe around her body and fold her into his arms.

The waitress was right.

It was beautiful.

CHAPTER ONE

"Wake up, brother. We're here." Angus woke to his brother's shoulder shake. He sniffed and stretched his neck to relieve the cramp from sleeping against the truck's window. He'd taken the first leg of driving while Patrick snoozed.

"Connor's place?"

He groaned and put his fingers to the knot at his neck. *Fuck, I'm getting too old for this.*

Patrick opened the glove compartment and pulled out a stick of Axe deodorant and a comb. "No, dumbass. Bevvie said they were goin' out for a bit tonight. Come on. I need to get out of this fucking truck and into a pretty lass. It is my day, after all."

The knot started to release under the pressure. "What the hell are you talking about?"

Patrick slipped the scented stick under his shirt

and swiped it under his armpit. "Angus, what's the date?"

Angus thought for a moment and grinned at his twin. "Aye, I see what you're saying. St. Paddy's Day."

Patrick grinned back as he ran the comb through his thick ginger hair. "It is our duty, no, our *obligation* to go in there to see family and make our presence known to this city in the biggest, loudest fashion possible."

Angus smoothed a hand over his head. The sides were shaved close, but the top and back he kept long. Both men had similar styles but wore it differently. It was the only way most people told them apart. Patrick liked his long hair loose and flopping to one side, while Angus preferred to keep his in a Viking braid on the back of his head. "Well then, brother, let's not keep the masses waiting."

Patrick tossed him the deodorant. "Good idea to freshen yourself a bit after ten hours of driving."

Angus caught the stick and applied it as Patrick got out and raised his arms to the night sky in a long, bone-cracking stretch. "Let's get this party started, brother."

Truthfully, Angus would be just as happy going to their hotel room and crashing for the night, but

Patrick would never dream of staying home on St. Paddy's night. Or any other night most of the time.

Home—a strange word to use when their entire lives had been spent traveling around the country working on job site after job site. From the time they could grip a hammer, they and their brothers and sister had worked the family business. That broke up a few years ago, and both Patrick and Angus continued to travel and work different crews and jobs. Home didn't really have a meaning for them other than cheap hotel rooms or renting a temporary crappy apartment.

The lights from the bar and sounds from the Irish band bled outside to the street. His second wind came when Patrick opened the door and stepped inside.

Patrick lifted his hands high, palms out, and spread his legs to take up as much room as possible. "Bow down, mere mortals! Patrick and Angus are in the hoooooouuuuuse!"

Angus smiled as he waited for his twin to get his ya-yas out. Of the two of them, Patrick was the party-seeker and more outgoing one. Angus followed and did his own share of partying with his brother, but without the same level of spectacle. They drank, sang, flirted, and picked up women together, but whereas Patrick lived and breathed to have fun,

Angus had his moments where he needed space away from people.

Not tonight.

"Patrick!" Beverly, his oldest brother's wife, hurried over to him. Melanie, the pretty blonde that Owen somehow had snagged, followed closely behind.

"Ah, me bonny sister-in-law! Please tell me you've come to your senses and ready to run away with me?" Patrick put his arms around the stout woman and squeezed her in an enormous hug.

Beverly hugged him back, then punched him on the shoulder. "Not a chance, little brother. You want a shot or a beer?"

His face feigned horror. "Lass, don't you know me? Both, of course."

Beverly turned to Angus and treated him to the same big hug while Patrick greeted Melanie.

"So good to see you two here."

Her words meant more to Angus than he could say. Beverly represented to him the mother figure he never had growing up. His own ma had died when he and Patrick were three years old. All he had were vague memories of a large woman who smelled like cookies and gave big hugs. "Good to be here. Real good."

He released Beverly and followed her to the bar. "I'm so dry, dust would go down easy."

Hugs, handshakes, and backslaps happened as the brothers loudly greeted each other. The bartender set two whiskey shots and two green beers for the newcomers. Patrick eyed the woman as he picked up the small glass in one hand and the beer in the other. Angus did the same. "Life, liberty, and the pursuit of happiness. *Sláinte!*"

"*Sláinte!*" Garrett, Connor, and Owen switched to beer. Glasses clinked and lifted. Patrick turned to the youngest woman who appeared to be a part of the group, and a big flirty smile plastered itself across his face. "So is your name Happiness?"

The woman giggled and ducked her head. Angus recognized the look in Patrick's eye. Always on the prowl for a new conquest, Patrick seemed to be on a mission to fuck as many women as he could. Fat, thin, older, younger, the only requisites were single and willing.

Angus took a swallow of his own beer. He wasn't exactly lily white in that area. Most of the time when Patrick picked up a woman for the night, he did too. They'd brought women back to a shared motel room and even tried switching up once just to see if the women noticed. They'd experimented with a few threesomes; however, that kind of kink didn't fly very long. Oddly, it was Patrick that put the kibosh on the practice.

"No offense, brother, but there's no pussy shortage out there. We can each get our own."

Angus agreed, but for different reasons. He and Patrick shared a womb and spent their existence as mirror images of each other, but they were two separate men. As such, Angus kept a few secrets to himself.

Melanie's voice broke into his thoughts as she pointed at his twin. "Don't you try anything with this one, Patrick MacAteer. You either, Angus." She turned to face the petite female. "Fair warning, sister. These two are the biggest horndogs God ever put on this planet. I wouldn't take anything they say seriously."

Patrick pretended to be hurt. He put a hand over his heart and made a gulping sound. "Shot dead. Oh, cruel, cruel woman! You'll dance over me grave at midnight, won't you?"

"Absolutely, if you fuck with my friend here."

Angus put his empty shot glass on the bar and took another big swig of beer. "Ah, now, lass. We won't fuck *with* your friend." The stink-eye Melanie shot at him should have burned him to a cinder. Melanie used to be one of the biggest party girls in Asheville until she became a mother and hooked up with Owen. Angus laughed and winked at her. No doubt she caught the subtle play on words.

He turned his full attention to the small brunette perched on the barstool. "What's your name?"

"I'm Rhyleigh Givens. Part owner of the yoga place, along with Melanie and Bertie."

Her hazel eyes met his. That was all it took.

Recognition.

Angus owned a special set of tools made from powerful earth magnets. When they turned the right way at the right time, they instantly attracted to each other and could not be separated, no matter how hard he tried. It took the combined strength of him and Patrick to pry them apart. Angus swore he heard the click of those magnets joining when he and Rhyleigh locked eyes.

Melanie could warn all she wanted, but Rhyleigh just became his.

She saw it too, in the widening of those incredible orbs and the sudden intake of breath. She reminded him of a rabbit caught in a hunter's gaze. A combination of wonder, excitement, and fear reflected back to him. His groin tightened as he imagined that same look when she was underneath him with his dick buried deep inside her.

"You're Bertie, then? Garrett's Bertie? Nice to

meet you. Connor tells us you're not a raving lunatic bitch like the last one."

Patrick's question caught Angus's attention, and he broke the stare with Rhyleigh. The woman standing next to Garrett smiled and stuck out her hand. "Yes, I'm Bernadette, or Bertie for short. And no, I'm not a raving lunatic. Bitch only when necessary."

Angus chuckled as he sipped his beer. Garrett's life had been rough this past year as he'd tried to make a relationship work with a woman who did more taking than giving. He finally broke it off and had recently gotten involved with a new woman, Bertie.

Conversation continued around him, including an attempt from his twin at flirting with the bartender, Sloane, which she was quick to shoot down. When Patrick leaned over the bar and started talking to Sloane, Angus let the conversation flow around him as he sipped his beer. He took the opportunity to move and stand next to Rhyleigh, close enough he could smell her fresh clean scent, something light and floral.

"What does a yoga instructor do? Teach classes and shit?"

Her throat bobbed as she swallowed, and Angus noticed the jump in her pulse. He had the urge to put his tongue to that spot and taste her rapid heartbeat.

She inhaled sharply, as if just remembering to breathe. "I do a few classes at the community college right now. The studio is just getting started, but I'm planning for a lot of classes, groups, and private coaching. I work at Trader Joe's part-time, but I'm hoping that once the studio takes off, I can work that full time." She tentatively smiled at him. "It's been my dream to do this for a long time. Ever since high school."

He sipped his beer. "How long ago was high school?"

Her laughter came out like silver bells; pure and light and with a touch of underlying relief. "If you're asking how old I am, I'm twenty-seven. I tried the college thing, but academia and I don't mesh real well. I used to do a lot of sports like volleyball and gymnastics and kept up with some of that through the adult league at the Y. My leg and shoulder tendons started giving me trouble, and my physical therapist told me about yoga. Been doing that ever since. It's kind of an obsession now. You know? Getting healthy and staying that way?"

Angus leaned in so she could hear him better and to see how she reacted to his closer proximity. He expected the mundane conversation had relaxed her impression of him, and he wanted her off-balance a little longer. "I eat my veggies and burn a lot of calories just being in construction, but I'm not one to restrict myself from enjoying life's offerings." He lifted one of the colorful Irish Flag drinks Sloane poured for them and offered it to her. "Maybe you should indulge once in a while too."

He was sure she got the meaning behind his words. "Um… I already had one and I'm driving. So…." Her voice trailed off as she lifted one elegant shoulder.

"One more. I'll take care of you."

She took the shot with a smile. "Okay, but only this one. Got it?"

He nodded and smiled with approval. Even though she looked like a tiny kitten attempting to spit, she still took the drink when he pressed her. If she protested a second time, he would have backed off and regrouped. Unlike his brother, the chase was the part he loved the most. The longer it took, the better the win. He watched as she downed the drink. She huffed at the burn and he fished a couple of ice cubes from the cooler near his hand. "Here." He held one to her lips.

"Thank you." She tried to take it from him, but he moved it back from her grasp.

How far would she let him push her comfort zone?

"Let me. Open up."

The cubes dripped from his fingers onto her shirt as he put it back to her mouth. Those hazel eyes widened at him, but she parted her lips and allowed him to slip the two cubes inside. The kitten sheathed her claws. Satisfaction filled him as she crunched on them. "I'm not much of a drinker."

Melanie's announcement grabbed his attention. "We have a babysitter who's probably watching the clock about now. Love that you guys are here. Talk business and shit. We'll see you tomorrow at lunch, yes?"

Patrick bounced up. "Party poopers, the lot of ya. Come, me true loves, dance with me before I grow roots." His twin grabbed a surprised Rhyleigh from her perch and pulled her with him, snagging Bertie along the way. "My beautiful new girlfriend, please don't leave me!"

Angus ground his teeth at the interruption but then relaxed and let Patrick have his fun. There were plenty of women at the bar, and if Patrick stayed true to form, he'd be sampling as many as he could before settling on one.

Rhyleigh wouldn't be it.

He sat with his brothers as they commandeered a free table. It was hard to hold any kind of conversation while the band played. Patrick hopped on stage to join them, singing "The Rattlin' Bog" at the top of his lungs. The audience loved it and gave him a big round of applause as he took an exaggerated bow and jumped from the stage. Bertie returned to Garrett, leaving Rhyleigh with the jumping mess Patrick called dancing. She kept up for a while and matched him dance for dance, but she gave up after several other women joined them. She came back over to the table, her beaming face shining with sweat as she breathed heavily.

"That's it for me, guys. I have an early shift tomorrow."

Connor looked up. "Are you safe to drive home?"

She nodded. "Yeah, I didn't drink all that much, and I just burned through what I did. Your brother has more energy than anyone I've ever met."

Angus stood up from his chair. "You sure?"

"Positive."

"I'll walk you out."

"Oh, you don't have to do that. My car isn't too far."

He smiled at the renewed game. "I'm not asking, darlin'. I'm walking you out to your car. You'll get in it and drive home. When you get there, you're going to text me to tell me you got there safe. Understand?"

Her lack of protest told him volumes. She nodded in agreement. "Um… okay. I'll need your number."

"Open your phone and hand it to me."

She did, and he quickly programmed his number. A moment later, his phone beeped from his back pocket. He took her elbow and steered her to the exit. As they left, he slid his hand to hers and grasped it firmly. She stayed by his side and let him lead her.

"My car is over there."

"Got your keys?"

She handed him a set with a fob, and he beeped open the locks. When they reached the car, he pulled her around so her back was to the door.

She looked up at him with wide eyes. The dim streetlight reflected the bits of green floating in the brown of her iris. She shivered as he deliberately tested her personal space.

"Thanks for walking me."

Her voice was steady enough, but Angus noted with pleasure the increased pulse in her neck. "No problem. I wouldn't be much of a man if I let a pretty woman go to her car by herself, especially from a pub full of drunk, happy men. Safety first, right, darlin'?"

She gave a short laugh. "I guess so." Her lower lip folded into her teeth as she dropped her eyes from his. "Am I safe with you?"

His gaze focused on her lips. "You're always safe with me. Mind if I ask you something?"

"Sure."

"Are you married or have a boyfriend?"

Her laugh came out again. This time with a nervous tinge. "No. I've got too much to do for that right now. Why do you ask?"

"Because I don't want some jackass coming after me for doing this."

He wound her long loose hair around his hand and used it to tug her head back. She gasped at the pull and he took the opportunity to cover her open mouth with his. His tongue speared inside, and he slanted to deepen his reach. She let out a half-groan, half-whimper as he stroked her mouth. He sensed her acquiescence when she raised her hands to clutch at his work shirt and relaxed, allowing him free rein. He explored her mouth, drawing her tongue out to taste and to play. *Sweet! So fucking sweet!*

Her tentative touches sent bolts of electricity to his groin and his dick swelled. He got the impression she wasn't a virgin, but not exactly experienced either. The thought of teaching her something of himself? *Intoxicating.*

He kept hold of her hair while he ended the kiss with one last tongue touch. His mouth hovered over hers and he felt the quiver in her lips and her panting breaths. "Remember the instruction I gave you?"

She swallowed before answering. "Yes, I do."

"Good. Get going, sweetheart. I'll be waiting for your text."

He watched as she got in the car on wobbly knees and drove away. Normally, on a night like tonight, he and Patrick would be out on the prowl for a good time and he would take the pleasure offered. With his good looks and practiced lines, he easily found willing women to spend the night in his bed.

The taillights of Rhyleigh's car flashed red as she paused before turning a corner. So why didn't he push her? She was pliable enough that just a bit more effort on his part, and she would have been under him until tomorrow morning. It was that magnetic pull. He recognized it; she didn't and it would take time to plumb the depths of the attraction. Delicious, seductive, time. Angus licked his lips and tasted the remnant of their kiss. Sorry, Melanie, but there was no way he was through with Miss Rhyleigh Givens.

The sight that greeted his eyes when he reentered the pub had him let out a huge guffaw. Patrick stood on a table, hand over heart, and sang "Oh Danny Boy" while the cute bartender filmed him on her phone. He hammed it up like crazy as usual, but there was care in his voice. Patrick had been by Angus's side since birth and seldom had they spent time separated from each other. Patrick lived life in the moment, relishing in a variety of wine, women, and song. Angus knew more than anyone else, there was more to his brother than a good party.

After the first verse, Angus glanced over at his brothers and saw Connor swipe under his eye. Random memories of his childhood floated through his mind. The times when all five brothers sang around campfires or on the long road trips. Growing up in a working family meant TV and video games weren't readily available. It was second nature to him and he joined in, singing the next verse. Connor and Garrett stood to bring their own voices to the mix. Owen seldom spoke because of a lingering childhood speech impediment, but he could sing.

Angus's heart clicked again. When the family business blew apart several years ago, and everyone scattered to find their own way, he never thought he'd be singing with his brothers again. That part of his life was over and he'd had to accept it. Now seeing all five of the MacAteer brothers together again, singing in rich harmony, he realized he and Patrick had come home.

It felt good. It felt right. It felt like he found the place he was meant to be, even though he hadn't known he was looking.

They finished the song and even though last call had come and gone, Patrick's charm helped to score them some unopened beer bottles to take with them.

The bartender handed them out and Patrick twisted off the cap to take several huge swallows. Angus tucked his bottle in the crook of his arm, intending on drinking it back at the motel. A quick glance at his brother and by the glazed look in his twin's eyes, he figured on driving as Patrick was on his way to being too drunk.

As they left and headed down the street, his phone buzzed in his back pocket. One corner of his mouth curled up as he saw the text from Rhyleigh.

Rhyleigh: All safe and sound. 😎

Angus: Good. Sleep well and have nice dreams.

Rhyleigh: 😴

Angus: Like that, is it? You talk in emojis very much?

Rhyleigh: 😉

Angus: You said you have an early shift tomorrow. When do you get off?

Rhyleigh: Around three, but that could change depending on who shows up late. 🎉

Angus read her reply and wanted to text that she could get off with him anytime, but he held back. If he came on too strong, he would spook her, and she'd run from him and his plans. He and his semi-staggering brother made it to the truck, and Patrick handed over driving privileges to Angus without protest.

Angus: What's the rest of your schedule this weekend? Have any time for me?

Rhyleigh: I don't think I can fit you in.

Angus barked a laugh. Too easy. Did she realize the opening she gave him? He resisted the temptation. The last thing he wanted was to come on too strong and scare her off.

Angus: Pity. I'd love to see you sooner rather than later. Sometime next week?

He put his phone in the dashboard clamp and set the GPS for the motel. Patrick had already wedged his head in the spot between the seat and the door and gently snored. With his mind still on Rhyleigh, the drive to the cheap hole-in-the-wall they'd booked was short. And receiving several more texts from Rhyleigh, he may have put his foot down, eager to get there so he could read what she'd said.

Rhyleigh: I'm on nights next week. Sorry.

Rhyleigh: My life is kinda complicated.

Rhyleigh: I probably shouldn't have kissed you like that.

The motel they booked was so old the beds were doubles and not queens. Patrick dropped his duffle bag on the floor and entered the bathroom. Angus heard him peeing as he left the door open. He laid back on the cheap flowery polyester cover and read through her messages a second time. Already she was nervous around him and making excuses. Angus smiled. Any other women he would have deleted the string and forgot her name. Rhyleigh had no idea the appeal she exuded and the potential she had. Christ, he loved this part of the game! He texted her back.

Angus: Yes, you should have. I intend on doing it again as soon as possible, and you're going to let me.

His thumb hovered over the Send button, and then he retyped his message. Best to keep it casual for now and keep a softer tone. If he came on too strong, she'd run for the hills.

Angus: I kissed you, sweetheart, and I'm glad you let me. I hope you will again.

The three dots stayed inert for a few seconds, then bounced around.

Rhyleigh: Perhaps. If you're a good boy. 💋

Out of the corner of his eye, he saw Patrick come out of the bathroom in nothing but his jockeys and scratching his balls. His brother let out a huge burp that resonated in the cheap room before he flopped face down on the second bed. Angus heard a drunkenly muttered, "Sloane," before Patrick passed out.

Angus ignored him.

Angus: I'm very good. Now go to sleep like the good girl I know you are. Dream of me and I'll talk to you soon. 😎 🛏

He got up long enough to finish his nighttime ablutions and settled into the view of the cracked ceiling plaster. Patrick's snores rattled the room, but Angus was used to the noise. He put his hands behind his head and his eyes traced the lines overhead.

Christ, it was good to be here! All three of his older brothers had found happiness in this mountain city. Beverly was perfect for Connor. Melanie fit Owen like a glove. Garrett and Bertie were new, but if the looks in their eyes were any indicated, theirs would be a long-haul kind of couplehood. His sister, Eva, found her peace not too far away in Bryson City and so far had produced four girls in her marriage to her biker husband, Stud. Hell, even Patrick sounded different as he actually remembered Sloane's name. His twin never paid enough attention to learn who he was flirting with and often called his temporary partners "love" or "darling."

This might be it, Angus mused, picturing Rhyleigh face just after he kissed her. *Only one element is missing and I'll find that soon.*

CHAPTER TWO

"I need to get my hair done and go shopping this afternoon."

My mom made the announcement at the breakfast table while I made one of my chocolate protein smoothies and sat at the kitchen bistro table as she stirred berries into a bowl of vanilla yogurt.

The unspoken part of that sentence was "I expect you to come with me."

I sucked up some smoothie before reminding her I already had plans. "I'm meeting Jodie at the studio this afternoon to iron out a few more details before the grand opening. After that, I have a shift at the store."

Unspoken: "I'm sorry, but I'm already busy."

True to form, the lines around my mother's mouth stood out as she puckered her lips in irritation. "I thought you'd join me and we could have lunch."

Unspoken: "You never have time for me."

We'd played this game for so long, it had become a habit. She'd make hints but refuse to come out and say anything directly, then silently sulk if I didn't fulfill her wishes. Sometimes, I'd cave just to preserve the peace, and sometimes I had obligations that I had no choice but to keep. My job was one of them, and she hated it.

When the pressure of her silence rose high enough, she'd explode at me with whatever vitriol she'd built up, using every perceived slight from the past as a weapon. The problem? She didn't yell or scream her way through a tantrum. That was too gauche for a woman of her standing. She'd use words in carefully placed sentences, specifically designed to flay the skin from her victims. In some ways, that was worse than taking a beating.

The lines stayed present as she sat near me in her fluffy white robe. She maintained her hair appointments meticulously, so she always had the perfect golden blonde color and her nails done in a tasteful French manicure. My father was a provost at the university and had some community standing. Appearances had to be maintained at all times, as you never knew who was watching.

The image was supposed to be of a big happy family with successful and well-adjusted kids.

That image faltered a bit when it came to me.

"Your sister is coming."

Unspoken: "You should cancel your meeting."

"That's great. Please tell Deidre I said hi, and I'm sorry I couldn't make it today."

Unspoken: "I really can't cancel."

I sucked the rest of my smoothie down and rinsed the glass in the sink before putting it in the dishwasher. "I have to go. Enjoy your day, Mother."

She spooned her yogurt and made a humming noise.

Making my escape, I grabbed my gym bag from my room and left through the basement. I supposed some people would consider it pathetic I lived with my parents at my age, however my finances didn't really allow me to go anywhere else right now. College didn't work for me, mostly because I didn't know what I wanted to do. I had no career plans and no direction and didn't see a point in taking random classes until I did. After three semesters, I tried to go out on my own and moved into a two-bedroom apartment with three other women. My résumé proceeded to collect a wide variety of jobs as I searched for something to make into a career. I'd worked in a restaurant as a waitress, a clothing store as a bra fitter, a clerk at a gas station convenience store, a cashier at Walmart, and a nighttime cleaning crew for offices.

The space was tight in the apartment, but we'd managed to get along and make it work for a few years.

Then one of my roommates started bringing her boyfriend, Ken, over. He slept there several times a week, and when he did, I ended up on the couch in the small living room so he and Gemma could have "private" time. He was cute and nice, and at first, I liked him a lot. We'd talk and joke around while Gemma got ready for their dates, and I didn't mind when I didn't get to stay in my half of the room. Then came "the night."

I was snoozing away when I felt my legs being spread apart. "Wha's goin' on?"

"Gemma's got her period. Stay quiet or we'll get caught." Ken pulled aside the crotch of my panties and went down on me.

I could've easily stopped him, and I was sure if I protested, he would've left me alone. The truth was, I wanted it to happen.

Gemma hadn't figured out that sound carried, and every time she and Ken got together, the rest of us knew it. Each time, my other roommates would roll their eyes and complain about the noise. Me? I'd listen and picture in my head what they did. It made me flush with heat and an unfamiliar desire. It also filled me with shame, as I wasn't supposed to want my roommate's boyfriend. Every time I heard them having sex, I imagined it was me instead of Gemma. I would lay on the sofa and touch myself, thinking about what it would be like to have him inside me.

The one and only time I was with Ken, I gave him my virginity. The next day, he ignored me like nothing happened. A week later, Gemma had a major meltdown one night, crying hysterically about Ken and how he cheated on her any chance he got. She never said my name, and I got the impression she didn't know about Ken and me, but the guilt was so bad, I started looking for another place to live.

Minimum wage didn't go very far in Asheville. It took two jobs to make ends meet, and even then, they didn't line up real well.

When I'd mentioned this to my older sister, my mother called me within the hour, insisting I should come home.

"It's embarrassing that you're living in that tiny apartment with so many other people. If you have to do that find-yourself-thing, then do it here."

That was seven years ago, and after a wider variety of different jobs, I still hadn't "found" myself.

The only bright spot was yoga. One of my

various jobs was at the Y as a desk clerk, and I got to use the facility for free. I fell in love with yoga and had been studying it ever since. Becoming a certified instructor became a reality for me, and I started teaching classes at the Y instead of just taking them.

Maybe this was a life calling, or maybe not, but it had become a big part of my life and had led me to this group of women who were more like sisters to me than my own family.

I pulled up to the studio and saw that Jodie had already arrived. She had an iPad in her hands and was taking inventory of the clothing line we carried. Health and wellness products like drink powders and supplements sat in shipping boxes ready to be shelved. I'd help with that task until I had to teach my ten o'clock class. I had three sessions today and later, a few hours at the grocery store. The studio started out strong and seemed to be growing at a fast-enough pace. Soon I'd be able to quit the store and work here full time. The class schedule made working hours odd and time consuming, but the potential of turning my passion into a career filled me with hope and excitement.

"Hey, Rhyls. I got another six people on the waiting list. That makes a full twenty looking to find spots, so we really need to look at adding another class. There's been a handful asking about early morning sessions. You up for that?"

If it meant I could move out of my parents' basement at last, I'd make it work. "Sure. Are we talking 6:00 a.m.?"

"Probably. We should have some showers installed so people can take the class, then get ready for work."

She put the iPad down and stretched her arms above her head. "Jeez, I need a break. Bertie is dealing with that shit from last week and still has her hands full with her inn; otherwise, I could use her help here."

I picked up a box of protein bars and walked over to put them out on display. "You got me for a couple of hours before the masses show up."

"Cool beans."

We worked in the front of the store listening to a playlist of new age instrumental music. My preference was old 80s and 90s pop-rock, but Bon Jovi or Nirvana didn't exactly help to keep the Zen atmosphere I needed for the studio. My mind drifted as I folded and set up the display boxes and stacked jars of protein powder. It had been roughly two weeks since I'd been at Gallaghers's and met Angus. He texted me several times since just to say hi or to ask about my days. He mentioned getting together for a drink at the pub, but I hadn't been able to find room in my work schedule to meet him. It bothered me some as I did want to see him, but my priorities at this time revolved around advancing the studio so I could move out of my parents' place and my mother's thumb once and for all. He would probably lose interest soon and move on to greener pastures.

Still, each time his name popped up, my stomach twisted into anticipatory knots. That kiss had burned into my memory, and I remembered every small detail. The firm tug on my hair, just shy of pain. His demanding tongue as it ravaged my mouth, thrusting in deep in the act of penetration—the flavor of his lips as he took complete control of me. I'd had to grab his shirt to stay upright as my knees weakened. My clit had electrified, and if he'd touched me there, I would have gone off like a firecracker.

The experience excited me and scared the shit out of me at the same time.

I had to stop thinking about it as I needed to get a few minutes' quiet time to center myself and prepare for the class. This one was designed to promote stress release, and I giggled at the irony of wanting a different kind of relief. I got my mat settled and sat in a lotus pose to go through several minutes of breathing.

In through the nose over four, hold, and out over four. Round the back. Relax into yourself.

The class progressed well. I designed it for more beginner work and used a lot of basics, but I was still satisfied at the end of it. The other participants smiled with their own satisfaction as they got up to leave. My heart beat steady and strong in my chest, and my muscles were warmed and relaxed. I loved it.

My phone chirped with a text message. *Angus!* My stomach fluttered as I picked up the glittering rectangle and opened the messaging app.

Angus: Hi, how are you?

My middle bloomed with heat. So much for relaxation and Zen moments.

Me: I'm good. Completed my first class of the day. You? .

The three dots bounced around.

Angus: Just finished a deck job and have a rare afternoon off. Want to grab a coffee somewhere?

Me: I don't drink coffee.

Angus:

Me: I can get a tea while you get your coffee. But I can't today as I have more classes coming up and I have to work tonight.

Angus:

Angus: That's a shame. I really want to hang out with you sometime.

Me: Sure. 👍

The three dots sat still as I watched them for a minute or two. I guess that was all I was going to get. I wondered if he meant it about hanging out. In the past, I'd had more than one experience of a man saying they would do something and not follow through. Dinner at a nice restaurant, a promised outing, a favor for a favor, sometimes they'd show and sometimes not. I'd make a vow to never fall for some cute line a guy fed me, but then I'd end up at a table all alone, anyway.

"You look happy. Got a hot date?" Jodie came back in the studio to grab some price tags out of the storage closet. A few ladies came in to set up their mats and chat a bit before the next class.

"No, just a text from a… friend."

"Hmm. You know, my husband, Jerry, has a single guy down at the car dealership about your age. Real nice and great manners. I can get him to introduce you."

I chuckled and shook my head. "I appreciate it, but not now."

"Next weekend?"

I knew Jodie's tenacious nature. Sometimes this was a good trait to have and other times it would get a little too much. "Maybe. I don't know my work schedule yet and I… uh… have to work late at Trader Joe's on Friday night."

"How 'bout Saturday afternoon? You can do a lunch date after the morning class over at that deli across the street."

She would not let up until I caved. "I'll try."

"Great. I'll get Jerry on that tomorrow."

Gratitude filled me when the bell rang over the door, indicating there were people coming in the studio. Jodie dropped the subject of my singlehood and rushed to help them. More women came in and filled the room for the second class of the day, and I needed to get back to my preparations. This one was a bit more advanced and difficult than the one from earlier. I took three long, cleansing breaths and pushed aside the tension that appeared in my shoulders and the thoughts of Angus from my head.

This proved to be harder than usual.

I led the class on autopilot, moving from pose to pose, guiding the people through the stretches and breathing routine, but my head wasn't in the game. No matter how deep I inhaled or how loose I tried to make my muscles, there still remained a stirring in my gut. A restlessness that pervaded my body and my mind.

Tension with my mom over shopping and lunch didn't help.

As I finished out the hour, another text chimed, and that same thrill hit me about Angus. It wasn't a message from him, but it sent sparks flying through me, anyway.

Text: Entrer dans Le Donjon. Oui ou Non?

I glanced around to make sure no one watched me and typed in *Oui*.

The return text simply stated the date, location, and an invoice.

My hands shook a little as I paid from my private PayPal account. It had been quite some time since I'd done this, and perhaps I needed it more than I thought.

CHAPTER THREE

I DIDN'T LIE TO JODIE AS I REALLY DID HAVE TO WORK late on Friday. My shift ended around ten, though, which gave me plenty of time for my other activity.

I drove to the location with my bag behind me, gripping the steering wheel with white knuckles. The address sat smack in the middle of an industrial area. Plain square buildings and a few warehouses stood on either side of the long road, and very few lights were around. I parked as far back in the lot as I could and sat in my car for a few minutes to calm myself and get ready.

I didn't indulge this side of my nature very often and participated even less. My preference was simply to watch, and I carried plenty of guilt over that wish. The few times I tried to participate ended up being disasters, and I didn't really want to try again, but I couldn't stay away.

A couple approached the designated building, and the doorman looked at their phones for the entry code. They wore long trench coats that no doubt concealed something darker underneath. I glanced down at my work uniform of khaki pants and Hawaiian shirt. Based on past experience, I'd stick out in this crowd, and more attention would be paid to me than I wanted; therefore, I needed to change into my different persona.

I exited my car and looked around to make sure I was alone. Only the crickets and cicadas sounded in the night. I shimmied out of my pants and hauled on the tight black leather-looking tights. My shirt and bra were exchanged for a black leather corset with laces in the front and cloth cups to cover my breasts. I added my flat-heeled boots—not knowing if I'd be standing or sitting. Lastly, I wound my hair around my head and put on a page-boy black-haired wig. It was obviously fake, but that didn't matter in this setting. A black mask and black lipstick finished my disguise. Now, I was ready. Or rather, my alter ego, Tacet, was ready.

I stood next to my car and debated. Part of me wanted to go home while the other part trembled with excitement. A loud motorcycle pulled up in the lot, and the rider got off in full black biker leather to enter the building. The doorman checked his phone and let him in.

My phone said it was 11:15 p.m. If I wanted to see this show, I had to go in now. I took a long, relaxing breath and walked toward the entrance.

"Enter the dungeon?" the doorman asked me. I didn't trust myself to speak as I showed him the code. He smiled behind his mask and opened the door.

I entered into my dirty little secret—one my friends and family knew nothing about. One that had fascinated me since the night years ago when I'd snuck out of the hotel with my best friend and two contraband tickets. One that made me feel abnormal and filled me with shame at my fixation with it.

I told myself over and over again that I should not want to be like this, but I couldn't stay away. I had to give into this dark impulse and feed my obsession.

I appeared more conservative compared to many other people here. Latex and PVC lingerie, harnesses, corsets, garters, and stockings, all types of fetish clothing that revealed breasts, asses, and dicks. I kept my eyes from lingering too long for two reasons. I wanted to give some privacy to the people engaging in their activities, and I didn't want anyone to approach me with an offer to join them.

I still got to see plenty as I searched for the private show area: a woman giving a blow job and hand job to two men at the same time. A man spread eagle getting flogged while strapped to a St. Andrew's cross. Another woman being taken in the ass against the wall. I passed several open scenes until I found the area I wanted to see and why I paid for the ticket to be here.

A Shibari show.

This was the reason I kept a membership to this club. The other BDSM activities had their appeal to some, but it was the ropes that drew me. My private guilty pleasure and the reason I adopted my other self, Tacet.

I found a spot in the upper balcony to the left of the staging area where I could stand in relative isolation. The view was dead on the harnesses draped from the scaffolding, and I watched the participants from above.

From the start, disappointment and irritation filled me at what I saw on the stage. The woman already had several coils around her body and thrashed her head as her partner continued to loop and tie around her. He made a big deal of grabbing and binding her hair in the rope weave and forcing a ball gag in her mouth. It looked over-the-top and fake. A show just to put on a show with no meaning and no intimacy between them.

The ties did not look artfully placed but twisted around the woman's body with no real pattern. When he hoisted her in the air for a suspension, she looked off-balance and in pain. It was all wrong, and I hated it.

"Bad, isn't it?"

My heart nearly jumped out of my chest at the close voice in my ear. It pounded so hard and fast I thought I would die of a sudden heart attack. I hardly ever spoke or interacted with other people at these events. To have anyone sneak up behind me sent shockwaves of panic through my veins. I needed to get it together.

I pulled in my inner peace and took several deep breaths to compose and calm myself.

You're Tacet tonight. Just Tacet.

"Yes, it is." *There, that sounded normal. I think.*

The heat from the man who stood behind me danced over my exposed shoulders and the back of my neck. I couldn't help the wince that came from my mouth as the woman's neck got wrenched back at a sharp angle by the ball gag.

The man behind me said nothing but made his own grunt of disgust.

A light woodsy scent mixed with leather and something else drifted to my nostrils. I looked down at where I gripped the rail in my hands and saw worn black leather motorcycle gloves holding on either side of them, boxing me in. He was taller than me by several inches and gave off an aura of power that had me intrigued and intimidated.

"I'm Tacet." *Damn, why did I do that?* I handed him what amounted to my private club name. That created the possibility of him asking me for a scene, and I didn't do that part of this life.

"I'm Conspiciens." His voice was low, and the timbre resonated in my head. This would be a name I'd remember forever. Another Latin pseudonym, meaning *he watches*. Perhaps his goal was the same as mine.

I held my breath as he moved closer and his lips whispered against my ear. "Nice to meet you, Tacet."

That was it. That was all he said before he moved back a few inches. Butterflies still ripped through my stomach, and I took a few more cleansing breaths to make them go away. It didn't work.

The man made another sound of disgust when the rigger jammed a giant purple dildo between the woman's open legs. "I'm done with this crap. This is not what I came to see."

"Me either. I think I'm going to leave." I fully expected him to ask at that point for a scene, and I ran through a dozen excuses in my head.

"You go first and I'll watch you get out of here safely. I'll leave in twenty minutes to give you time for a private exit from the parking lot. Deal?"

I didn't expect that. Relief flowed through me and I nodded in agreement. "Deal."

Cooler air brushed over my shoulders as his heat moved away. I stifled a shiver at the loss. The path to the door was relatively clear, and I left the same way I came in, keeping my eyes behind my mask, to myself. Once I reached my car, I ripped off the wig and let down my hair. I kept a stash of baby wipes in my gym bag and used three to clean the makeup and lipstick from my face. I doubted my mom or dad would be awake at this hour, but I never took any more chances than I had to.

My eyes rose to the entrance, and I debated on waiting to see if the mystery man came out like he said he would. A scene might distract him, or something else grab his attention and I would sit here for hours waiting. Curiosity filled me, but lots of people who came to these events had an expectation of anonymity. I decided to let him keep his as he had honored mine and drove away.

Angus caught sight of the red taillights as they turned out of the lot to follow the road to the main route. He removed his own mask and picked up his helmet.

Fuck me sideways.

He still had trouble believing his eyes. Rhyleigh had come to this private club event. She had worn a disguise and used a pseudonym, but there was no doubt the pretty shy yoga girl had been there. He had already decided to leave the shit show when he'd spotted a woman across the balcony platform, hiding behind a pillar.

At first he hadn't recognized her, but then she'd pulled her lower lip into her teeth, and her identity hit him like a tidal wave. His dick stretched long and hard in his black jeans and he had to adjust it several times as he approached her. The show kept going, but his eyes stayed on her and her reactions to it. And when her mouth drew up into a moue of revulsion, he'd chuckled at the sight.

During their whole exchange, she never turned to face him. If she had, she might have called him out.

He didn't care one way or another about club names or masks, but they made some people more comfortable to have that thin shield. He could understand the need as his own family had no idea of his interests. Not even his twin knew about this side of him. It wasn't that he was ashamed or anything about his preferences. He simply believed this part of his life to be private and had no need to share it with them. If Patrick did find out, Angus was sure his brother would shrug it off and probably ask to join in.

Maybe not, Angus thought as he kicked up the stand and started the bike. Patrick had taken to hanging out and working at Gallaghers's Pub a lot lately. It was a crapshoot if he did it for the party times he loved so much or for the cute bartender with the ever-changing hair colors.

He jammed the helmet over his head and tightened the strap as he glanced in the direction those taillights had gone.

"I think I'm going to leave."

"You go first and I'll watch you get out of here safely. I'll leave in twenty minutes to give you time for a private exit from the parking lot. Deal?"

"Deal."

This encounter was burned into his brain just like that kiss from a few weeks ago. He'd texted her several times and asked to meet her at the pub, but her work schedule hadn't left any good times. After tonight, he had no idea if he could sit across from her as Rhyleigh on a barstool and make small talk while imagining her as Tacet.

Fuck me sideways, he thought again and pulled out onto the road, his head full of Rhyleigh and the way she gnawed on her lip.

CHAPTER FOUR

I avoided it as long as I could, but eventually, I gave into my mother's demands for a luncheon at the country club with my sister. I wasn't fond of these command appearances, but I seldom got to spend any time with Deidre unless I attended. Sometimes they were wonderful, and I had a great time with my family. Occasionally they consisted of my mother complaining about anything that currently annoyed her, my sister bragging of her latest big house sale, and both of them asking me when I was going to get my act together.

This last scene happened more often lately, and based on the huffiness of my mother's mood, I expected today to be a session of Rhyleigh-bashing.

Deidre walked in, perfectly coiffed in a plain but stylish dress and modest heels—the epitome of a successful businesswoman. Mom wore one of her standard conservative pantsuits. Me? Nice shorts, matching shirt, and flat sandals. I could tell by the line of her mouth that my mom disapproved, but I didn't know what exactly she expected. I didn't have an office to go to, or clients to impress. Work attire for me consisted of loose yoga pants or leggings, and sports tops, or Hawaiian shirts and khaki pants. Not exactly haute couture.

Just get through lunch and get to the studio, I thought to myself as I smiled and prepared for a long hour.

My sister smiled with her perfect billboard teeth that sold hundreds of houses. "Hello, Mama. So good to see you, Rhyleigh."

"You too, Deidre."

She leaned down to press her cheek briefly against mine and Mother's. "You're looking well, sweetheart. Make any big sales today?"

Deidre sat and placed her purse on the extra chair. My old gym bag sat on the ground in contrast to the designer Coach bag. "Yes, I did. Remember that lovely little house in Biltmore Woods? The stone one? We received an offer this morning. Fingers crossed."

The soft Southern lilt of Deidre's voice might sound cultured and charming to most people, but it was only a matter of time before that pretty drawl turned razor sharp. Deidre had the ability to sound sticky Southern sweet while at the same time, slicing deep with targeted precision. Just like our mother taught her. "So, Rhyleigh, you still playing around with your little yoga hobby?"

I gritted my teeth. "It's not really a hobby. I've actually become a business owner with a group of women. We've opened a studio on West End Boulevard and it's getting great reviews."

"You've opened a business. Oh my Lord in heaven, how long will this one last?" Her tinkly laugh scraped across my ears, and I flushed.

"A lifetime is the plan."

Mom jumped in as water glasses and pretty decorative salads were placed in front of us. "Well, you have to understand where we're coming from, dear. You've taken so many piddly little jobs over the years and still don't have a career. Deidre and I are just a little concerned that this latest scheme of yours will go the same way all the others did."

Deidre spread the linen napkin on her lap and smoothed it over her skirt. "Are you even making enough money to live on? Mama tells me you're still working at that grocery store."

I ducked my head. "I'm still there right now, but the studio is expanding and—"

My sister's waved hand cut me off. "Well then, until you can actually make a living, your little studio is still just another hobby. It's a nice one, but a hobby nonetheless."

Mom shook her head. "If only you had finished school and earned a degree, you'd be much better off now. Like your sister."

The urge to get angry warred with the urge to cry. This was my mother's favorite barb to throw at me, and she did so whenever she could with bull's-eye accuracy. "Not everyone is cut out for college, Mom. I'm sure Deidre didn't start out of the gate as a top real estate agent. The studio is going well and I'm hoping it will turn full time very soon."

Another dismissive hand wave. "We'll see."

That was Mom's way of saying she no longer wanted to talk about it. "So, Deidre, maybe you and Lawrence can come by the house after services on Sunday? Your Dad and I would love to meet him again and get to know him a bit better."

Deidre beamed her award-winning smile again. "That sounds lovely, Mama. Will you be there, Rhyleigh?"

I hadn't met my sister's boyfriend yet, and I didn't want to. It would be another rub-in-Rhyleigh's-face about the success of Deidre's life and the chaos of mine. "No, I'm sorry, but I have to work at my little hobby."

"On Sunday? That's disgraceful to work on the day of rest. What are you thinking, Rhyleigh?"

I didn't reply. There was no point, as whatever I said would be wrong. Deidre and Mom talked about what to serve at some upcoming charity event at the club, while I picked at my chicken salad. It was covered in slimy canned peach wedges, which made my stomach turn. I let their conversation drift over me. As long as the subject stayed away from my faults, I could get through this lunch and destress by spending some time at the studio.

Deidre's phone chirped, and she swiped to read the text.

"…take Rhyleigh shopping…"

The snippet caught my ear, and I perked up. "What do you mean take me shopping?"

Deidre sat back. "My word, Rhyleigh, haven't you been listening at all? The summer art gala my company sponsors each year is coming up in a few weeks. I'm on the planning committee for it and I need everyone to make a good showing. Surely you can fake your way through it."

White fear zapped through me. "Oh God, please, no."

Mom put on her sternest face. "Now that's enough, missy. You will attend with your family in support of your sister, and you will not show up in some scrappy vagabond Goodwill knockoff."

"I don't do well at those events and… "

"This is not a discussion."

My phone sounded a text, and I automatically looked at it.

"Rhyleigh, how can you be so rude? Texting at a dinner table is bad manners."

Wide-eyed, I looked at Mom, nonplussed. "Deidre just answered hers. Why is it rude of me and not her?"

Mom sniffed. "Hers is business, and yours is probably one of those yoga people."

"My yoga people are business people."

"They aren't on the same level as us."

And there it was. The snobbish attitude finally showed fully. "You know Melanie Miser, right? Her family belongs to this club, and she's both a client and an investor."

Deirdre tossed her head and crossed her arms. "Seriously, Rhyleigh, you're going to compare that tramp to us? Her family has a lot of money and are members here, but she works as a public school teacher for Pete's sake."

Mom started in on a new target. "You know she got herself pregnant, and now she's with some blue-collar construction man? I bet he never finished high school, and people say he can't string three words together without tripping over his tongue. Her mother is so embarrassed. I haven't seen her in weeks."

I had enough. I'd gotten to know Melanie through the studio and the classes she attended when she could. I'd seen firsthand the love that fierce woman had for her child and the devotion to her man, Owen. Rich or not, she didn't have a pretentious nature, and I was proud to call her friend. It bothered me that my mother and sister could be so shallow. "I need to get going. How much do I owe you for lunch, Mother?"

"I put everything on your father's bill. Besides, I know you don't have money for this kind of thing."

Back to the sweet-sugar smile.

Even though cheek presses and air-kisses were expected, I couldn't bring myself to do them. No doubt Mom and Deidre thought me rude again, but I had to get out of there before I exploded in anger or collapsed into a blubbering mess.

The latter was more likely than the former.

Once I made my escape and made my way to my car, I took a breath of the heated summer air and pulled up the text I'd received at lunch.

Angus: Hello, beautiful lady. Patrick and I are heading over to Gallaghers's later. Care to join us?

Warmth bloomed in my stomach. If only he knew how much I needed those words.

Me: I have classes to teach until eight, but I can come by after. Would that be too late?

Angus: Hahahaha! We'll just be getting started. See you then. 😄 😎 😂

Me: Anyone else coming by?

Angus: Don't know. Garrett might, but he's a homebody now with Bertie. After all the shit they went through, don't blame them. 😱

I agreed. Bertie had a nasty encounter with her ex-husband's new wife, which ended up with him getting shot and her going to jail. The woman had developed this weird idea that Bertie wanted her ex back and had gone mental over it. Absolutely ludicrous, as anyone who saw Garrett and Bertie together could tell they were meant to be together.

Me: I don't either. What a pile of 💩

Angus: 🚽

Me: 🧻 💩

Angus: 🧹 💩

Me:

Angus: Hahaha! You win. See you tonight!

The negative vibes from the afternoon lunch disappeared with the thought of seeing Angus at the pub.

A new text beeped with its special tone. Another one? I leaned on my car door and opened the text. The familiar message popped up.

Text: Entrer dans Le Donjon. Oui ou Non?

I typed in *Oui,* and words appeared that sent my heart rate through the roof.

Text: One night only, Mr. and Mrs. Johnson.

A date and time was sent along with a PayPal link. I'd go to this show even if it meant bankrupting my account.

CHAPTER FIVE

Gallaghers's was packed when I arrived. It looked like the whole city of Asheville suddenly developed a thirst for Irish beer and karaoke singing. I supposed I should have been nervous entering the crowded place, but I spotted Angus close to the entrance. He waved at me and smiled. "Glad you made it. Sloane is counting people and hoping she doesn't have to start turning anyone away because of fire code capacity."

He offered his hand, and I laughed as I took it. "I hope not. This place is nuts tonight."

"Yeah, it is. Loud as hell too."

His palm firmly grasped mine, and he led me into the building and found a spot near the back corner of the bar. No stools were free, so he put me in front of him and placed his hands on my shoulders, forming a human shield between the other patrons and me.

It was a nice courtesy, and I liked it a lot.

Patrick stood behind the counter, pulling beers, and Sloane mixed drinks nearby. She gave me a head toss as a greeting. I beckoned at Angus to come closer and he lowered his head to present an ear to me. I hoped he heard me enough as I didn't want to shout and add to the volume any more than necessary. "Is Patrick working here now?"

Angus's mouth was very close. It wouldn't take much effort to lean in and meet those beautiful lips with mine. "Yes, he is. Temporary help for Sloane and her brother. He likes it a lot."

"He looks happy."

"I think he is. He's found a place where he fits in perfectly. That means a lot to him."

Sloane drifted by and swiped the surface in front of us. Her hair coloring tonight was black and pink, and her eye makeup matched. "Hey, Angus. I expect you'll get a Guinness, right? What about you, Rhyls? Beer or something stronger?"

Patrick chose that moment to raise his hands in the air and give a huge yell above the crowd. "Who wants a Penis Colossus?"

The high-pitched female roar back deafened all

three of us. Sloane winced and gritted her teeth. "Fuck me, I hate that drink, but it sells like crazy."

"What drink?

She rolled her eyes. "The recipe Patrick made up. It's kinda like a Creamsicle shot but comes in a six-inch test tube glass. See that woman over there? Her name is Reese, and she renamed it to Patrick's Dick for the seven-inch tube. I'd ban it from the menu, but the women buy tons of them every night."

"I'll get a raspberry margarita instead."

"We have peach margaritas on special tonight."

I wrinkled my nose. "I don't like peaches much."

Sloane swiped again. "No problem. Raspberry it is. I'll put some extra sugar on the rim for you."

Patrick waved at us with a huge smile and kept working his adoring fans. A bunch of people got up to dance and the stool nearest us became vacant. Angus grabbed it and planted my butt there, still hovering close as he kept one arm caging me in.

"Good day?"

Sloane placed my drink in front of me on a paper coaster. With a nod of thanks, I picked up the glass and sipped at the sweet drink, noticing she made it extra strong. "For the most part, I guess. Classes went well and Jodie told me sales were up on the supplements and stuff. I had to deal with my mom and sister today, but I'll get over it."

He took a swig of the dark beer and somehow didn't get a foam layer on his upper lip. "What do you mean get over it? Did something happen?"

"Nothing really."

"Doesn't sound like nothing."

"It's just the normal drama whenever we get together."

He took another sip. "Family can always get complicated. I have three older brothers, a twin, and a younger sister. I bet I could write a book about all the drama we've had growing up the way we did. Hell, it could be a series."

I laughed and licked a bit of the crystal sugar on the glass rim. "I have an older sister, Deidre, who is beautiful, successful, poised, all the things I'm not. My mother will sometimes remind me of this, and she kind of did that today."

"Sounds rough. You okay?"

"Yes, for the most part. It does get to me once in a while."

"Does she know you have a part in a fast-growing business?"

I shrugged and turned the glass around and around on the coaster. Little rivulets of condensation fell down the sides and I wiped them with a finger. "They don't consider being a yoga instructor a career move. Deidre calls it my hobby and Mom thinks I should have finished college."

The noise from Angus's mouth had me looking up. His green eyes danced with amusement rather than disgust. "None of my brothers or me have college degrees and we graduated high school by sheer luck. I'd say with the number of work requests we have coming in daily, we're a pretty successful group."

I took another drink and caught an ice cube between my teeth. "I think you and your brothers are outstanding."

He smiled. "I think you're outstanding too. Education is a great thing, college degrees, and all that. I'm not knocking it. Some people find their place in a big office or in an operating room, and there's nothing wrong with it. For them. Other folks find themselves working with their hands or mixing drinks at a bar. It's all valid as long as you're happy with your choices."

I fished out another cube and was surprised to see I'd finished the drink already. "What if you're still looking?"

"One year or ten years, doesn't matter. Just so you get to where you're going."

I was a lightweight when it came to alcohol and

the strong drink hit me pretty fast. I had to suppress a yawn behind my hand and did my best not to show the world a view of my tonsils. "It's been a long day and I have another one tomorrow. I think I'm done for the night."

"Can you drive?"

"I think so."

Another yawn tried to fight its way out. He *hmphed* and pulled me off the stool. "I'm going to take you home."

"You don't have to do that. That's so much trouble."

He tipped back my chin and his eyes locked to mine. "You're never trouble, Rhyleigh." His lips lightly grazed over mine and the electric shock took away any other protests I had.

He paid for our drinks and took my hand. The air outside the pub breathed thick with humidity, and I noted silently that rain would come soon. He led me to a motorcycle of all things, and I smiled in delight. The mountain roads were magnets for bikers, and I'd always wanted to know what it would be like to ride one of these powerful machines. Angus handed me a helmet and showed me how to strap it on. Its weight rested heavily on my head and made it awkward to move around. He mounted the bike and pointed out the places I needed to put my feet. Excitement built in me as I settled in behind him and pressed in close.

"What's the address?" His voice came out muffled as he punched at the GPS screen between the handlebars. After I told him, Angus started the engine, and it rumbled between my legs sending low vibrations through my body.

Before I could acknowledge the sensations, we took off.

He negotiated the city streets at a sedate pace, but when we hit the highway, he opened up, and we flew. The wind rushed past as we sped along the road. It was glorious. I let my hands slip further around his middle, under his jacket to the front of his stomach. The play of his muscles worked in tandem each time Angus shifted gears. Man and machine worked together in smooth coordination, and I loved the balance between them. Biker Zen moment, perhaps? I smiled under the helmet, wishing this ride would last forever.

All too soon, we pulled up to the dark house. A frisson of embarrassment started in my brain. What was I thinking? What would he think of me, finding out I still lived at home with my parents? At my age, I should be out in the world, earning a living in an established career.

I scrambled off the bike and nearly landed on my ass. "ThanksfortherideIneedtogo," I blurted while my fingers pulled at the straps under my chin.

"Here, sweetheart. Let me." He reached underneath and with a few gentle tugs, freed the tangle I'd made. Tears burned behind my eyes at the tenderness of his touch.

"What's wrong?"

"Nothing."

"Rhyleigh." Despite the soft word, the command was clear.

"I didn't want you to know I still live with my parents at my age."

He reached out and traced my jaw with his fingertips. "I've never lived alone either. Always had my brother around, day and night until recently. It's strange to go home to an empty house."

You wouldn't be alone if you took me with you. The words flashed across my frontal lobe and nearly came out of my mouth. He smiled, and for a moment, I thought perhaps I *had* said them aloud. His hand slipped to the back of my neck, and he pulled me in to take my mouth.

The kiss was more exploratory than demanding. He drew my lower lip between his and lightly sucked, stroking the edge with his tongue. "Open, baby." I did, and he took over, teasing and tasting with leisurely thoroughness. Something let loose, and warmth flooded my belly. My breasts grew heavy, and my nipples tightened into points against the restraints of my sports bra. I had the desire to rip it off and see what Angus's reaction would be to my naked form. I wasn't that well-endowed and on the thin side. Would he curl his lip and walk away, or would he draw me into his mouth and ease the ache in my body?

I didn't get the chance to explore that thought further as the porch lights snapped on, and a figure peered from a side window.

"Guess that's my cue, darlin'. Text me tomorrow and I'll take you back for your car. Maybe get a bite of breakfast on the way."

"You're kinda bossy, aren't you?"

He shifted on his growling bike and gave me an unapologetic smile. "Yes, I am."

He waited until I had the door open before he pulled away from the curb. I turned inside, fully expecting my mother to be standing there ready to berate me. Instead, I saw my father. His gray hair stuck out in all directions, and his eyes were on the fading red taillight of the bike.

I held my breath, but he said nothing. The noise

of the bike decrescendo-ed to silence before Dad finally turned to head back upstairs.

"Goodnight, Rhyleigh."

That was it. I didn't think he cared much, but at least he spoke to me. "Goodnight, Dad."

I made my way to my own room and got ready for bed. Angus stayed in my thoughts as I drifted off.

CHAPTER SIX

THE FRONT ROOMS OF THE CLUB SAT ALMOST EMPTY. No surprise there as an appearance of Mr. and Mrs. Johnson would have the big stage area packed to capacity. I still elected to find my spot in the upper viewing area and paid extra for the privilege. I wore my same disguise and kept to myself as best I could. The crowd hummed and anticipation thickened the air to the point I could taste it.

Angus had picked me up and taken me to my car like he said he would, but I hadn't seen him since. His work schedule made mine look like vacation time, and all he managed to do was text me a few times. My mother grilled me about "that man with the motorcycle" my dad mentioned, but so far, I'd kept her in the dark from knowing his identity.

Tonight, I was in my own alternate persona for

this show. The rigging at my view seemed more complicated than what I'd seen years earlier. A web of knots, rings, and pulleys hung to the stage with multiple points of suspension. My mask slipped a few times as the heat from so many bodies rose, and I began to sweat. I looked at the other people surrounding the catwalk-like balcony area. Person after person met my eye briefly, but no one was recognizable in their attire. Even if I saw Conspiciens, I wouldn't know him. I never saw his face when I met him, nor did I see his mask.

The lights dimmed until only the stage was lit. I peered across the upper balcony and saw nothing as the dark shadows deepened, making the people there disappear into the black depths.

A hush fell over the crowd as the couple came to the stage. They were older but no less charismatic. Soft music started playing, and the show began.

It was just as I remembered it.

The lights, music, colors, and background all looked exquisite, but it was the loving care he showed to his wife and her full trust in him that made me want to weep.

"Hello, Tacet. Beautiful, isn't it?"

The word reverberated through my middle as Conspiciens came up behind me. I hadn't realized how much I wanted him to be there and to join me.

"Yes, it is. Hello, Conspiciens."

He made a noise and moved to stand right behind me. The same heat that radiated from him at our first meeting hit my back, and I shivered despite the warmth of the place.

"Cold?" he asked and his breath brushed my bare shoulder.

"Not at all."

He stayed silent, but the aura he put out powerfully drew me in, and I became more aware of him as the show continued.

Coil after coil, loop after loop, knot after knot, Mr. Johnson tied his wife. Every movement done with a caress by gentle hands just as I had seen it years ago. Her face wore an expression of ecstasy and love. His showed deep care, and the intimacy between them became so tangible, I thought I could have touched it.

A finger came up and wiped a tear that tracked down my cheek. "Are you okay?"

His whisper sounded gruff in my ear. I hadn't realized I was crying. "Yes, I'm fine. It's just… It's…."

"You don't need to explain, Tacet. It's that connection between them that makes this art. That shitshow we saw before would never compare to this."

He pointed at the rigging and I noticed his hand clad in fingerless biker gloves. "See the double rings on each of the three pulleys? That is always a requirement in their performances for safety. She needs to feel secure, and he makes sure he fills that. Watch why this is important." My eyes drifted to the stage as my breath caught in my chest.

In one smooth, controlled movement, Mr. Johnson hoisted his wife in the air. Her head and body fell back into a cradle web of rope.

"See? No awkward swaying. No hesitation. No jerking from discomfort or pain. She simply gives it all to him and he treats it like the gift it is. It's rare to have that level of trust, which is what people really come to see. It's not about sex at all. It's about the total release of yourself to someone and having the faith they will treasure it."

He was right. Connections of this magnitude were extraordinary and matchless. The beauty of it made my heart long with yearning to find such a joining for myself and the odds of it ever happening.

The show continued with the puppetry of Mr. Johnson posing and spinning his wife, using the elaborate rigging to pull her body into arches, twists, and a variety of positions. His hands stroked her body as if she was made of the finest porcelain. More precious to him than anything else in the world.

More tears fell from my eyes, and Conspiciens lightly brushed them away. "Permission to touch?" he rumbled in my ear. At my nod, he placed both hands on my shoulders, and the cool leather contrasted with the heat of his body as he stepped closer. He pulled me back to him until I rested against his body. His hands traveled down my arms to rest flat against my quivering stomach, securing me to him. The craving in my heart moved to my stomach and lower down. Even if I didn't have what the Johnson's did, I could pretend for a while.

I watched as Mr. Johnson moved behind his suspended wife and did the same, letting his hands stroke over her body in an act of worship. Conspiciens hand curled into the cup on my corset and pulled the cloth down, exposing my breast. I gasped as open air hit my nipple, and it tightened into a point. His head dipped to kiss the skin below my ear while his palm opened over my flesh to massage the heavy mound. "Tacet," he whispered as his thumb and two fingers leisurely rolled my nipple between them.

A smoldering fire started low in my belly, burning embers that had me pressing back into the mystery man behind me. My head fell back to his shoulder, and a low moan broke from my mouth as his teeth nipped into my neck. Every muscle in my back shoulder contracted with exciting thrills, and I gasped again. His other hand moved up to free my other breast and toy with that nipple. The smolder turned in a blaze, and I writhed against Conspiciens like a cat in heat.

"Will you do a scene with me?" he whispered hoarsely. "No flogging or spanking or that kind of thing. Not even penetration. Just a simple binding and letting me make you feel good. Private room. No voyeurs." His fingers danced over my nipples, sending shooting stars to my clit. "Only condition I have is you'll wear a blindfold. Not for anonymity as much as trust. Will you trust me, Tacet?"

My body ached, truly ached, and his words promised release. "Yes," I breathed.

"What's your safe word?"

Safe word? I'd never thought I'd need one. Both sets of fingers rolled my nipple simultaneously, and my knees almost buckled with the pleasure.

"Peaches," I sobbed.

His hands released my breasts, and he moved away briefly. A long cloth came over my head and he gently tied over my eyes. "The trust starts now."

He lifted me up as if I weighed nothing. My arms slipped around his neck, and his scent flowed over me. I felt each step he took away from the show. The soft music faded and slowly got replaced with the harder pulsing beat of the main room. That too faded as he took me into the back halls. Ones I'd never been in.

We finally stopped, and he dipped down to open a door and enter what I assumed was a private room. He set me on my feet and steadied me facing forward. The room smelled of cleaner and spice and man.

"Permission to touch?" he asked again.

I nodded, not trusting my voice to speak. He chuckled and kissed the strip of my forehead between the blindfold and my wig. "You have to say it out loud, baby. The room is private and the cameras are off, but there are staff who listen to what's happening. Just to make sure everyone stays safe. If they hear something bad going on or permission is not granted, they will come in and stop the scene. Permission to touch?"

"Yes."

"Safe word?

"Peaches."

"Confirmed."

His fingers pulled at the closures on my corset, opening it and pulling it off. It made a soft thump when it hit the floor. The air in the room wafted over my bare flesh and I shivered. I heard some wisping sounds, and a moment later, his hands without the gloves passed over my shoulders and down my arms to my wrists. He brought both behind my back and folded them on top of each other. This made my back arch a little and my hard nipples grazed against his shirt. The embers in my stomach flamed again.

I didn't know how he did it, but somehow he bound my arms in that position. I tried twisting a little. The knots were tight and allowed very small movement, but no pain came from them. His hands came to my waist, and he squatted down as he peeled the leggings from my legs, taking my boots off at the same time. His touch traveled up and he kissed just above my bare mound.

"Pretty."

Another rope came around me and slowly wound around one thigh. A second one mirrored the other limb. With each coil, I pictured his fingers expertly weaving the rope in and out of itself, binding me to him in a way that was more than physical. I'd never reached this level of intimacy in the two brief relationships I had in my life. Probably because I didn't trust them with this part of me. I hinted once to the last man I dated about this need of mine and he made fun of it, calling it weird. Since then, I'd stayed away from relationships, and chose to simply watch. This was the first time I'd taken a chance and gone this far. My body trembled with anticipation at the unknown.

"I'm going to lift you and put you on the bed."

I think he knew I'd not done this before and the

extra care he took in communicating with me helped me relax. He scooped me up, and I felt the bindings more acutely. A moment later, he rested me on a soft, flat surface. "Comfortable? Any pain or knot digging in anywhere?'

"I'm good. Nothing hurts."

"Good."

A silky slithering noise sounded and my legs were pulled back high at the knees, spreading me wide. Even my buttocks opened up and exposed the most intimate part of my body to him. I couldn't help the cry that burst from my lips at the movement.

He paused to see if I would shout my safe word.

I didn't.

His fingers stroked between my legs, making my clit flame up and my body burn. They slid through the wet, right down to my anus. Another moan came from me at the forbidden touch.

"Anyone ever take you here?" he asked, probing gently.

"N… No." My voice sounded husky and foreign.

"I promised you no penetration today and I keep my word. I hope you'll let me be your first here."

I had no idea what to say to that. Then he put his mouth to me, and all thoughts vanished.

His tongue ran over my straining clit, teasing it with exquisite expertise. He licked it flat and sucked it into a point, while his fingers held me open. His breath blew across me before diving in to taste more. He flicked the very tip until I thought I would go mad.

I gasped, twisted, begged, and fought against the ropes that held me under his power. Waves of pleasure battered me but never quite crested. My empty pussy contracted, desperately wanting to be filled.

"Please, I need…. Ah!"

"What do you need, baby?"

"I need… I n-need…."

"I'm not putting my dick in you today. Do you want my fingers?"

"Yes! Please!"

He smiled against me. "Since you asked so nicely."

A long, thick finger pressed inside my channel, and I clamped down on it as his tongue twirled around my clit. More whimpering cries burst from my mouth as the pleasure built. Never had I experienced this height and never had I wanted to come so much. I was on the verge of shattering into a thousand pieces, and only he had the control of making it happen.

His finger pulled from my channel and stroked between my butt cheeks to press against my untried opening. His whole mouth covered my clit, sucking it deep and flickering hard. The pressure increased at my ass, and his slick finger slowly slipped inside.

I screamed as I came harder than I thought a body could. Wave after wave crested and broke free. I lost control of everything and let it go unchecked, trusting that Conspiciens would catch me in this freefall. Blood rushed to my head and overwhelmed everything in me. When I finally came down, I found myself so full that tears flowed from my eyes.

"Tacet?" Concern tinged Conspiciens's voice.

"I'm wonderful."

My anus burned a little when he withdrew his finger. I sensed him move over me and his breath tickled my lips as he leaned in close. I heard sounds and realized his hand pumped up and down on his dick as he hovered close. It didn't take long until long shots of thick, hot liquid coated my stomach and breasts.

"Fuck," he declared as he came.

We lay there for a while until our panting breaths slowed, and heartbeats resumed a regular rhythm. He kissed my neck tenderly as he shifted off me and began to unwind the ropes from my body. My legs came down, and he massaged the large muscles. I was sure my skin bore some marks from the tight wraps but nothing severe or bruising. The sensation of being unbound from the bondage echoed the release of my orgasm. Control was slowly restored to me as each coil came off. I felt more opened up. Freer than I had been before.

Conspiciens cleaned himself from me with what smelled like baby wipes. "I'll get dressed first and leave. Then you take care of business. I'll watch you as you leave to make sure you're safe. Understand?"

Something in his voice resonated with me, a depth I'd never heard before. A sense of déjà vu as if I'd been here before. *Angus?* The name crossed my mind, but I fast quelled it. What did that say about me if I dreamed of one man after sharing an intimate moment with another? "Yes, I understand."

He finished quickly, then helped me sit up. His lips pressed against that same spot on my forehead as he had earlier. "Thank you, Tacet. Both for trusting me and your gift tonight. I hope to earn more from you in the future."

He left before I had a chance to reply. I peeled off the blindfold and took a first look at my surroundings. Dim lights, possibly in deference to me being in the dark for so long. A pile of ropes, a couple of wood cabinets, and of course, the bed. My clothes sat folded neatly on a nearby footstool. My body hummed as I dressed and exited through the door.

People still milled around the main room even at this late hour. No one bothered me other than a few curious glances were cast my way. Could anyone tell I'd experienced the most mind-blowing event of my life? I ducked my head and hurried out the door as Tacet retreated and Rhyleigh came out, but it was a different Rhyleigh. My senses heightened as I got in my car and sat for a few minutes. I stroked my nipples through my clothes as I recalled the pull of Conspiciens mouth on them. My clit tingled in tandem and I had the urge to put my hand between my legs, imagining his head back there instead. I was more alive than I had been in years and at least for now, that was enough.

ANGUS WATCHED RHYLEIGH DRIVE OFF BEFORE HE started kicking his ass. *What the fuck was I thinking?* Taking her to a room had not been in his plans tonight, especially as Conspiciens. He hoped he was making progress getting to her as Angus and had vowed to stay away from her as his club persona until she could accept both. But when he'd caught sight of her there, standing in full view of the stage, he couldn't help himself.

Maybe it was the beauty on stage, maybe it was the air thick with pheromones, or maybe he just hadn't been laid in a long time. His dick had risen painfully high in his pants, and he'd had to touch her. Her scent in his nostrils, the sounds she made when he bared her breasts, the way she leaned back and gave herself over to him, he found himself driven to ask for the scene.

He seized his helmet from the back headrest and threw a leg over his bike. The memory of her snuggling into his back as she rode with him blended into the sight of her beautiful breasts framed in his knots. The blindfold was more for his protection than hers. He didn't have a clue as to how she would react to having Angus going down on her rather than Conspiciens. He licked his lips, recalling her sweet taste and the flood that poured from her when he'd fingered her ass.

"Peaches," he muttered.

He told her he wouldn't put his dick in her, because when he did, it would be as himself and not in a sex club. He wanted to look into her eyes—Rhyleigh's eyes, as he claimed her. His dick throbbed as he imagined how he'd take her pussy first and then her ass, making her all his and his alone.

"Fuck," he thought as he started his bike. "I hope I didn't fuck up."

CHAPTER SEVEN

"Yoga, eh? Is that some new-age thing where you burn candles and chant and stuff?"

I sighed. "No, it's not. It's actually been around for centuries and has more than one—"

"Hey, can I get some hot sauce over here?"

My mouth slammed shut as I vowed just to get through this date. Jodie obviously had no idea how to match people, as it seemed her criteria only included two items. Male and single.

I supposed Clint had his good points. He appeared clean and well-groomed when he met me at the deli this Saturday afternoon. Short-styled brown hair, blue eyes, nice build, and attractive for the most part, but no spark. The way this "date" was going, there likely wouldn't be any.

"So, Rhyleigh, what do you do for fun when you're not yoga-ing?"

"Well, I like to go hiking. There's some really nice trails up on—"

He cringed. "I hate hikin'. Too sweaty and my legs get sore. What else?"

"Um… I like movies. You know the film festival happens in—"

"I hate goin' to movie theaters. Too damn expensive with all the popcorn and stuff. Plus they all end up on HBO or Netflix sometime. Makes no sense to spend good money when you can wait awhile and watch for free at some point."

I took a bite of my Cobb salad. "I suppose you have a point."

"You like eatin' rabbit food?"

"I eat vegetables most of the time. I've considered trying—"

"Ugh, I hate vegetables. Give me meat and potatoes and I'm a happy man." He took a huge bite of the burger he ordered and grease dripped from it to punctuate his statement.

My irritation grew, both with Clint's constant interruptions and his list of things he hated. This included barking dogs, shopping malls, dentists, and mowing grass. Jodie had pushed me out the door earlier and waited at the studio for me to return. I had the feeling she would badger me for a blow-by-blow account and I looked forward to giving it to her.

"I hate it when…"

My mind drifted, and I stifled a yawn. This was Conspiciens's fault—he'd spoiled me for other men. He'd private messaged me twice this week through the club's system, and both times, I'd gone there to meet him despite the late hours and sacrificed sleep. The way he took over, manipulating my body as if he knew it better than I did became addictive, and I craved the next time he texted for an encounter.

"I have a present for you. Permission to touch?"

He tied me so my arms were behind my back, chest and head down, with my ass high in the air. My legs were bound against the bed and slightly spread. "Yes."

"Safe word?"

"Peaches."

"Excellent. You're so wet, you're glistening."

His words excited me more.

His fingers came to me and probed my anus. "I want to put something here. A training plug to get you used to opening up and being full when I finally take you." He slicked something cool and slippery against me. We agreed on no penetration, but apparently toys and fingers didn't count.

"This lube has some relaxing and numbing effects to help ease you into this. This is the tip of the plug. Ready?"

A hard object pressed against me. "Yes."

He pushed it forward, and I forced myself to relax. He pulled it back just as my ring started to burn and made short, slow strokes, advancing each time just a little further into my body. I panted as that part of me gave in to his persuasion. "Push out some and it will help. You're doing beautifully, Tacet."

The blindfold made the experience more intense.

"Almost there, sweetheart."

For a moment, I swore it was Angus talking to me and I wanted to call his name, but I promptly forgot about it as he firmly pushed the plug one last time. I cried out as my ring settled into the groove to hold it in place.

"Okay?"

I panted. "Yes, feels good."

"Let me make it better."

The muted whir of sound gave me a brief warning before he put the tip of a vibrator against my clit.

A flush crept over my neck as I realized I sat across from one man, thinking about another man I liked and the way a third man made me come—one whose real name I didn't know.

"Hey, did ya hear me?"

I shook myself. "Sorry, what did you ask?"

He sat back with a miffed expression on his face.

"You know, I hate it when someone can't keep their mind on their business."

I gritted my teeth. "I have a lot going on at the studio this afternoon."

The bell tinkled over the front door as new customers came in.

"I was sayin' if you want to go out again, that's cool, but I'll tell you right now, I only do dutch. A woman needs to pay her own way, if you see what I'm sayin'."

God, please save me! "I don't think... "

"Rhyleigh, my favorite girlfriend of all time! How ya doin', love?"

Apparently, God has a sense of humor in sending Patrick MacAteer as my guardian angel. He leaned over and kissed my cheek with an exaggerated *mwah.*

"I'm fine. This is... uh... Clint. He works with Jodie's husband."

"Nice ta meetcha, I'm Patrick, and this is my brother Angus."

My stomach dropped like a lead weight as two hands placed themselves casually on my shoulders. "Damn, you two look just alike." Clint's eyes darted between the two men.

"Twins do that sometimes. You one of Rhyleigh's students?" The voice above made me jump a little. Angus tightened his grip to hold me in place.

Conspiciens rang in my head, but I knew who stood behind me. I stilled under his control and kept silent.

Clint guffawed and sat back. "Hell, no. I ain't into any of that shit. I'm jus' doin' Jerry a favor to get his wife off his back. She's been tryin' to get me set up with someone for months. You ever meet that woman, you know once she gets a bone in her teeth, she ain't lettin' go."

Patrick laughed long and loud, slapping his hand on the table hard enough to make the plates and silverware bounce. "Fuck me, that's funny! Did you hear that, Angus? My best girl Rhyleigh's just a favor."

Clint's brain gears clicked into place as last. "You two datin' or somethin'?"

"Nah, dude. She's a good family friend, and we like to look out for our friend, right, Angus?"

Angus's fingers dug into my skin and his thumb traced the indentation at the very top of my spine. "Yeah, we do, Patrick."

Clint looked between the two brothers a few more times. "I guess I don't need to hang around and keep the lady compn'y then. Y'all have a nice day."

He left the booth and the deli. Thankfully, he grabbed his check and paid on the way out, not leaving it for me. Patrick flumped down in the spot that Clint had abandoned, and Angus bumped my hip until I shifted enough to let him sit next to me. His idea of personal space was sitting so close our thighs touched, and when I tried to move away, his hand came down to clamp on my thigh.

"Don't." His single word command froze me to the spot. He sounded angry at me and it pissed me off a little as I'd done nothing wrong, but I sat still under his hand. I decided to ignore him and give them both the famous Rhyleigh silent treatment.

Who am I kidding? I couldn't give anyone the famous Rhyleigh silent treatment. "I can't believe you two did that. Horn in on my date that is, but I'm kinda glad you did."

Patrick laughed as the waitress came up. "Oh, me darlin' girl. You have much to learn in the ways of men. That asshole came to Gallaghers's a while back and got real fresh with Sloane. Yeah, he was drunk as hell, but he put his hands on her. Now, you know we like a bit of drinking and a having a good time, but you lose control like that and possibly hurt someone? Not gonna happen on our watch."

I hazarded a glance at Angus's profile. His jaw flexed with his clenched teeth as his eyes perused the menu. He might be mad at me, but I had no doubt that if I needed him to rescue me, he would. "Jodie has been hounding me constantly about setting up this date with her husband's coworker. Maybe now she'll stop."

Angus's green eyes turned to me. "You couldn't tell her no?"

Their intensity burned me and it took me a moment to find the right flippant answer. "Have you met Jodie Harris? No is not in her vocabulary."

Patrick grunted. "I get that. Garrett told me she's a good woman overall, but can get obnoxious when she sets her mind to something. Bertie's had to lay into her about interfering with people's private lives. You'll have to do the same to get her to back off."

They placed their orders while I continued to pick at my salad. Conversation turned to business, upcoming jobs, class schedules, and other small talk. Even though Angus had let go of my leg, I remained acutely aware of him next to me. I didn't move away.

"You got anything special happening, love," Patrick asked around a fry he'd popped in his mouth.

"Not really. I have to go to a charity thing my sister's company is doing tomorrow afternoon, but that's it. Just work tonight and the studio classes."

"Bertie said the business has increased a lot, and you may be expanding sooner that you think. Something about the space next door opening up."

"Yes, that's the retail side of the place, but I'm not

as involved with that part. I just do the classes, mostly."

The body to my right spoke up. "A lot to keep up. You get a workout every class you teach. How many can you do per day without wearing yourself out?"

I put down my fork and faced Angus's questioning gaze. It seemed a casual inquiry, but there might be some underlying concern. Perhaps it was fantasy on my part, but I hoped he did have some care for me. This also brought guilt as I'd made time to meet with Conspiciens to the point of giving up sleep and had not done the same for Angus. "It depends on the type of class. Some are designed for stretching and flexibility. Some are more meditative for stress relief. Others are for calorie burning. I can do at least one of each every day, but you're right in that it might be too much if I added in the private sessions more people are starting to ask for. We may have to hire another instructor soon."

Patrick wiped his mouth with a paper napkin and sat back, man-spreading to take up the entire booth space. "How bendy are you?"

I smiled. "Bendy enough, I guess. There are some poses I haven't mastered yet, but I've been able to work into quite a number of advanced poses that I couldn't do a year ago."

"Can you put your elbow in your ear?"

"Trick question. That is a physical impossibility based on human bone and muscle structure. What I can do is a plow pose where I fold in half until my knees reach my ears or the fire log pose where my leg is lifted behind my head. Those are pretty tough to do and it's taken me a long time to get to this point."

"Hmm, maybe we should take some of your classes, eh, Angus?"

Angus threw a fry at his brother. "Like you have time? You're either on the job or working the bar with Sloane."

"Aye, I am, and I'm happy with it."

I picked up on the change in Patrick's voice, and from Angus's reaction, he did too. "You thinking about taking a trip to Vegas sometime?"

Patrick leaned forward to pin a serious stare at Angus. Brother to brother, eye to eye, mirror images of each other. "Yeah, I am."

I had no idea what that meant, but it was big apparently, as Angus reached a hand out for a firm shake. "Congrats, brother. I'm happy for you."

In the next moment, the serious vibe vanished, and all three of us finished up our meals and got ready to assume our work days. I unwrapped the complimentary Star Mint and popped it in my mouth. "This is great and all, but I need to get back to the studio and relieve Jodie." I nudged Angus as he finished typing a text on his phone. He slid out of the booth and picked up my check as well as his. "You don't have to do that."

"I know, but I'm gonna." He tossed his own Star Mint in his mouth and crunched down on it. I decided not to argue with him.

We left the deli and Patrick sauntered over to the dusty work truck.

Angus gripped my elbow and pointed me in the direction of the studio. "I'll walk you back."

"You don't need to do that either."

"Yes, I do."

His tone held no harshness, but it did hold command. I suppose some women would get pissed at his attitude, and might even find it smothering. Me? I didn't. In fact, I liked it.

Jodie grinned huge when I walked in. "How did it…. Oh, hi, Angus."

"Not very well. He walked out and left her to pay for her own meal," Angus said before I had time to respond.

Her face fell. "Oh, that's too bad. Jerry told me he could be a jerk sometimes, but I was hoping that… well, never mind." She got up from her spot behind the counter. "I need to get going. The kids have a late soccer game, and Jerry's gonna need some help with the concession stand. Call me if you need me to run back later, 'kay?"

She picked up her purse and gave me a brief hug before darting out the door. "Angus, I may need your professional opinion on the store next door. I'll set up an appointment for some time next week, all right?"

The doorbell tinkled, and she was gone, leaving me mildly amused.

I turned to Angus, and the air intensified. "I wish I had a third of her energy. That woman constantly... Oh!"

Angus pulled me behind the studio curtain and pushed me back against the wall. He didn't hurt me or slam me around, but it did startle me. "Angus, what... "

His mouth came down and his tongue drove inside. My senses filled up with all things Angus. The taste of Star Mint, the mandate of his hands, his body close against me, and the demand of his lips to yield.

And yield I did.

My arms came up to wrap around his neck and shoulders. His hands came down to lift and separate my thighs and settle them around his waist. The hardness of his body pressed into my core, and I whimpered as pure need rushed into my belly. Without thinking, I started grinding against him, seeking relief from the sudden fire between my legs.

Conspiciens. The name flashed through my brain again and shut me down faster than a dousing of ice water. I tore my mouth away and gasped for air.

What am I doing? It wasn't so long ago I had another man's mouth down there and allowed him to do things to me I'd never done before. Conspiciens had given me the most fantastic nights of my life, and I wished to do it again and again. I craved the night he would penetrate my body with his in all the places he said he would. True, I made no promises to him, nor he to me, but I still had a sense of loyalty to him. The problem was I had that same desire for Angus. Here and now, if Angus wanted to take me against the wall, I'd let him. I wanted to feel him naked on top of me, his hands and lips on my aching breasts, and that hard as steel dick inside me instead of against me.

What kind of slut had I become to want two men at the same time?

The bell tinkled as someone entered the store. Angus let me down and lifted my arms overhead to hold my wrists against the wall. His lips hovered over mine with familiarity. "No more blind dates." His fierce growl vibrated in my chest.

"No more blind dates," I repeated.

"Anyone here?" the customer yelled.

He released me and stepped away. "I know

you're busy this weekend, but you and I are going to have a talk next week. Make time for me."

"I will."

"Hello?" I needed to get to the person in the store. Two deep breaths and I walked out, praying my flushed appearance looked more like a recent workout than sexual arousal.

"Welcome to The Yoga Spot. What can I do to help you today?"

"Oh, there you are. I've been hearing about this flexibility class you have? Can you tell me more?"

The slightly overweight woman didn't notice when Angus slipped around her to leave. His parting look had enough heat in it that I had a hard time focusing on the woman's chatter. She signed up for the next round of classes and purchased three sets of workout clothes before she left. As soon as I was alone, I all but collapsed in the chair behind the counter.

Conspiciens-Angus-Conspiciens-Angus-Conspiciens-Angus.

My head ripened, ready to burst.

"Will do you a scene with me?"

"I hope you'll let me be your first here."

"What do you need, baby?"

"Do you want my fingers?"

"No more blind dates."

"You're never trouble, Rhyleigh."

I wanted to scream. Tears formed and spilled down my cheeks while I wrestled with myself. A light rain started to fall, which drove a few people inside to mill around and poke through the racks. I wiped my face with a tissue and bottled everything inside into a big ball. The problem was, I had no place to put it; therefore, it rolled around the edge of my mind.

A new text chimed, pulling my attention away.

Text: Entrer dans Le Donjon. PM Oui ou Non?

Private message? I sat at the desk for a few minutes, my gut quivering. I dreaded opening the text as I already had an idea about what it said.

Conspiciens: I'll be at the club tonight. Come to me.

Tacet: I have a late shift at work.

Conspiciens: Come after.

Tacet: I'm not sure.

Conspiciens: I want to see you.

I wanted to see him too. God help me, I wanted it badly. But Angus just held me to the wall and told me not to have any more dates. But it was Rhyleigh he ordered, not Tacet. Did that count?

Tacet: I'm not in a good place right now. I'm confused about a lot of things and need to get my head straight.

He didn't answer immediately, and I was afraid I'd made him mad. Then the three dots jumped around.

Conspiciens: I understand. I'll check back with you soon and we'll talk about it.

I couldn't tell if he had brushed me off or if he understood what I meant. Two more customers came in and I needed to refocus on the tasks at hand. I added more shit to the rolling ball in my head and fake smiled at them.

Angus exited the app on his phone and leaned forward in the truck seat to slip it back in his pocket. This shit had gotten way out of hand, and he blamed himself for letting it happen. After the first scene with Rhyleigh, he swore he'd not touch her again until he told her who he really was. But like a game-playing asshole, he invited her for another private scene and then another. He still hadn't actually fucked her, but he'd played with her body with an intimacy that some couples never reached.

"What's got your panties in a twist?" Patrick drove the truck and flipped on the wipers as droplets of rain sprinkled across the windshield. "Shit, I hope this shit dries up before we get back to the site."

Angus sighed. "Didn't like that fuckwad around Rhyleigh."

"Me neither. You gonna tap that ass soon?"

Angus didn't respond right away as his mind spun. He'd texted Tacet, but Rhyleigh responded. He told her no more blind dates as Angus and she'd listened when she refused to meet Conspiciens. Angus smiled in relief. She may not know for sure, but she'd made her choice.

"Planning on it." He looked out the window at the darkening clouds. "I think we're done for the day, brother."

CHAPTER EIGHT

THE DAY STARTED BADLY WHEN MOTHER BARGED INTO my bedroom this morning holding a pale pink dress on a hanger.

"We have to go to church this morning. It will look bad if we go to the party and were not seen at services."

"Whut?" I sat up while my groggy head did its best to make the connection about why church could be important to a party.

This prompted an impatient huff followed by a classic eye roll. "Hurry up, Rhyleigh, this is important for your sister and it won't kill you to help her out a little."

Deidre, one of the top agents in her company, needed my help? I shook my head to clear the cobwebs. Last night, I'd tossed and turned for hours, thinking about Angus, Conspiciens, the studio, the club, and whatever else my brain decided to torment me with. Pressure built up behind my eyes and I flumped in the bed with a groan.

This was a mistake.

"Rhyleigh, for Christ's sake, get up and quit your foolish drama!"

"My head really hurts."

"Take an Advil and get moving. I bought you this dress yesterday because I'm sure you don't have anything appropriate."

"I have dresses."

"Stop arguing and get in the shower!"

I shut my mouth, showered, and put on the dress my mom wanted me to wear. I didn't like pale pastel colors, and the style of the dress looked more like a potato sack with ruffles. The mirror told me I resembled a juvenile in middle school rather than a grown woman. However, if I changed into something else, my mom would unleash a shitstorm over me that I could not handle this morning. Better to take a pill and resolve to get through the day.

I should have taken two. Or three.

Church for my family had never been about religion or belief. It was expected for social standing and appearance. Christmas and Easter were guaranteed attendance, and other occasions cropped up from time to time when my mother deemed it necessary.

Our family arrived early enough to mingle, smile, and exchange a few pleasantries with other members.

"Oh, so good to see you!"

"Good to see you, too!"

"You look fantastic. Have you lost some weight?"

"Maybe a few pounds. Gotta watch out for those carbs."

"Oh, don't I know it. I have a terrible sweet tooth."

It was like running a gauntlet before I got to the pew.

Deirdre stood next to the long bench in her red and black power suit. She smiled and waved us over. A man in a dark gray suit next to her had his back turned as he spoke to someone. A frisson of danger buzzed my spine as I looked at the back of that dark-haired head. I stopped moving, and Mom pinched the meat of my arm, hissing at me through her smiling teeth. "What is wrong with you? Get that look off your face and support your sister!"

Support my sister? I had no clue what she meant.

We reached the pew Deirdre had kept for us and repeated the same casual Southern woman greetings we'd already said several times.

"Momma, Daddy, you remember Lawrence, don't you?"

Premonition, sixth sense, psychic power, whatever the title, it hit me. Something was about to happen that would rock my world like a train wreck, and there was nothing I could do to stop it. The tall man turned with a huge smile and greeted my parents with an extended hand.

"Nice to meet you. I'm Lawrence Kenneth Peak."

The last time I saw that face was on top of me as he pushed his dick inside my untried channel. Ken. Deirdre's wonderful boyfriend was Ken, who took my virginity when his girlfriend had her period. This was Ken, who gave me my first orgasm. This was the Ken I crushed on so shamefully hard. This was the Ken who tore out my heart and left it bleeding on the floor when he had what he wanted and ignored me after.

"So good to see you again, Lawrence. This is my other daughter, Rhyleigh." Mom pushed me forward, and I stumbled a step. "Oh, she can be a little awkward sometimes."

"Nice to meet you… Rhyleigh?"

Any hope of him not recognizing me flew out the window. His eyes shone with surprise and maybe a little fear before it hardened into a smiling mask. His hand extended, and I took it automatically. It tightened a little firmer than I expected, and I got the message from him—"don't fuck this up."

Deirdre's bell-like laughter interrupted, and she took Lawrence's arm. "My sister can get a little tongue-tied at times. Let's get seated."

If only she knew where my tongue had been on her boyfriend.

I managed to seat myself away from the happy couple. The service droned on for almost an hour and a half, and I found myself drifting. More than once, the sharp elbow of my mother jabbed me to attention.

"Wake up. You're embarrassing us."

The luncheon party took place right after the service. I declined the ride with my sister and Lawrence, not wanting to get any closer to him than I had to. Mom huffed and berated me all the way to the country club.

"Honestly, Rhyleigh. Your manners are atrocious."

I kept silent in the back seat and started my "it will be over soon" mantra. My dad, as usual, didn't say anything but just let her rant at me.

The club had a big enough crowd I could lose myself in it, but I didn't have that option. My mother demanded I stay right by her side. "We need to present ourselves as a family unit."

I still didn't get why, and I probably never would.

Deirdre reveled in this environment. She acted the epitome of a successful Southern businesswoman. Sweet as sugar but respected and ruthless in her career. She and Lawrence looked great together as a top power couple should. I faded into the background and tried my best to blend in, but my efforts weren't good enough.

"Stand up straight."

"Hold your shoulders back."

"Smile, for Christ's sake."

I gave up. One day soon I hoped the studio would grow, and I'd be financially solvent enough to move out permanently, but for now I needed to grit my teeth, keep the peace, and survive the day. "I need to go to the restroom." Any respite would do, even five minutes of hiding in a toilet stall.

"Hurry up."

The ladies' room had a lounge area in addition to the bathroom. A few stylish women were touching up makeup as I entered. They didn't bother to acknowledge my presence, so I went in to do my business. Snippets of their conversation drifted to my ears.

"Deirdre's in rare form today."

"I noticed. That promotion she's been after gets

announced next week, and if I know that woman, she'll get it. Did you see her parents are here?"

"Yes, and that big hunk of man she's dating too."

"Hard to miss that. What I wouldn't do to have her life."

I left the stall and moved to a sink on the far side of the room to wash my hands. More words came as I squirted some complimentary cucumber-melon lotion into my palm.

"Shame about her sister."

Wait, what?

"Deirdre has a sister?"

"Yes, and from what she says, the girl is an unmitigated disaster. Can't hold a job and still lives at home."

"Is she here too?"

"I don't know. If she is, just look for the most awkward and unfashionable woman around, and I bet that will be her."

I left the bathroom's rear exit with the thought at least they had no clue to my identity. My temples pounded with pressure, and I fumbled for the Advil packet I'd slipped into my mini purse and walked to the water fountain close to the back hallway.

"Rhyleigh."

Oh, shit! The packet dropped to the floor.

Lawrence approached me with a strange look in his eyes. "Um... hi... uh... Lawrence."

He closed in and immediately got in my personal space. I backed up until I slammed into a back wall. My heart rate picked up. Not in excitement but in fear. We were alone in a back hallway, and unless someone came through the restrooms on the other side, no one would see us. He leaned in close, and the sharp scent of his aftershave wafted over me.

"In case you need to know, yeah, I recognize you from when I dated Gemma. I remember the night I fucked you. Still can't believe I was your first."

"Yeah, you were." My knees knocked together, and I locked them to keep from shaking apart.

"You were such a hot little piece. So fucking tight." He raised a finger to stroke down my cheek. "Is it still tight?"

"I don't.... You shouldn't be talking to me like that. You're dating my sister now."

He blew out a laugh. "Your sister is a class-A bitch sometimes. Fucking her is like fucking a log. The only reason I'm still around is this promotion. If she gets it, I can ride her coattails to my own corner office. If she doesn't, I'll be looking for a new woman who can give a decent blow job."

His fingers moved down my neck and over my shoulder. I froze to the spot. Should I fight him? He was bigger and stronger than me. Should I scream for help? This far away from the party, no one would hear me. Should I walk away? I thought back to answer number one. He could easily overpower me and make me stay. "Please, stop touching me."

"Why? You asked me to touch you plenty that night. Your legs spread for me like soft butter back then, and you said over and over again how much you wanted me. I remember how eager you were to have me inside you, telling me you loved me, and were so happy I finally got with you. We could do that now. Just turn around and drop your panties. No one will ever know."

"I'd know."

"So? From what I've heard, you don't count for much in your family. Deidre told me her little sister was a surprise addition and not a particularly wanted one." He smiled in a friendly way, but the expression didn't quite reach his eyes. "If I were in your position, I'd be pissed as hell at my family and take any paybacks I could get. Wouldn't it be a kick walking back to the party full of my cum?" His hand drifted to cup my breast. "Never fucked two sisters in one day. How'bout another first for the both of us?"

Nausea rose in the back of my throat and I swallowed repeatedly to choke it back down. I'm sure my face was red from the flushed heat coursing through me. My heart pounded so hard, it rocked my entire body with the force. He seemed to notice it and mistook it for desire or at least acquiescence.

His smile changed to one of triumph and he started pulling my dress up. "Turn around, Rhyleigh."

Voices drifted from the other side of the restroom doors, and one started to creak open.

"Not that way, Vera. Over here."

The interruption shook me out of my stupor, and I broke free. I ran. Yes, I ran from that place and hoped I left that part of myself behind. He caught up with me just as I got to the main foyer. His hand grabbed my arm in a bruising, iron grip, and I yelped in pain.

"You say anything to Deidre or your parents, and I'll tell them it's all fantasy in your pretty little head. Who do you think they'll believe?"

He let me go and strode off to the party room, no doubt back to Deidre's side. She grinned up at him and possessively took his arm. He placed his hand over hers and looked down at her fondly as if there was nowhere else he wanted to be. They appeared to me as the perfect power couple. He was right. If I walked up to my sister and parents and told them what he had just done, I have no doubt who they would believe.

I wanted to leave, but I had no car, and unless I got desperate enough to risk my mom's wrath by calling an Uber to leave early, I had to find some steel for my spine. *A few more hours and it will be done.*

Three long, cleansing breaths later, I entered the party. Thankfully, Lawrence stood with my father on the other side of the room, while Mom and Deidre faced a painting on the wall. I came up behind them and opened my mouth to greet them when I heard part of their conversation.

"I wished you hadn't brought Rhyleigh, Mama. She's just so awkward in public. I hate my friends seeing her. It's so embarrassing."

"I know, dear. I probably should have left her at home." Mom gave a long-suffering sigh. "I don't understand her. She's had every opportunity like you did, yet she's wasted her life away on nonsense."

"I'm so sorry she's such a burden to you. If she wasn't such a failure, then maybe you and Daddy could've enjoyed his retirement by now."

Awkward. Embarrassing. Burden. Failure. Those words hit me like bullets. I didn't say a word to them or anyone else. Hurt couldn't begin to describe what burned in me. Betrayal came closer, but this fiery pain went further inside. So deep, it deadened every-thing inside. I turned and left.

I called for an Uber and sat under the portico while I waited. All the cleansing breaths and medita-tion in the world would not erase the repeated lines in my head.

"You don't count for much in your family."

"I hate my friends seeing her."

"She's wasted her life away on nonsense."

Numbness made it too hard to cry. The Uber pulled up, and I got inside. I started giving my home address, but did I really want to go there? Mom would be back in a few hours, and I didn't have to imagine how she'd barge in my room and ream my ass for leaving the party. Gallaghers's Pub wasn't open today. I thought about the studio.

Angus. You should call Angus. He'd meet you some-where and take care of you.

Then a text chimed on my phone.

Text: Entrer dans Le Donjon. Oui ou Non?

I didn't bother checking out the future show invi-tation or the participants. Instead, I gave the address to the driver.

CHAPTER NINE

I HAD THE DRIVER DROP ME OFF AT THE TOP OF THE road leading to the hidden club warehouse. The kitten heels made walking on the gravel road diffi-cult, and I stumbled a few times. I'd never come here this early, nor for anything other than a Shibari show. Also never in a pink dress that made me look like a schoolgirl out on an adventure. I showed my text code to the bemused doorman and entered the club for the first time as Rhyleigh. Not Tacet.

The thumping music came at me with a harder punch than normal. Not as many people were around, but more than I expected. I swallowed and finally directed my gaze to some other patrons and openly stared at them. A woman in a breastless corset, boots, and G-string led a naked man by a studded collar. One man sat at the bar with his woman and fondled her breasts. Another sat at a table with a slave at his feet and her head bobbing in his lap. Two women sat on their knees in the classic submissive position. Their arms raised to rest at the backs of their heads and knees apart in "display" while their Master sat between them, drinking something from the bar. They definitely noticed me.

A man approached me. He was big, brutish, and decked out in leather pants with a codpiece shaped like a huge dick and a leather hood that had eye and mouth holes. "You lost or curious?"

Lost came to my mind. What my mouth said was "I've been bad."

The man grinned. "Follow me."

I did. My head pounded with hammer-like blows, and my stomach roiled. I wanted to throw up. I wanted to run. I wanted to announce this was a mistake, and I needed to go. Instead, I followed the big, strange man to a room. Tacet didn't walk into the club, nor Rhyleigh. I wasn't sure who came to this place for this purpose or what kind of headspace she occupied. The person in the pink dress was someone I didn't know and scarier than the torture looking devices in the room.

"Let's get this party started."

I let him push my front against the St. Andrew's cross. My legs were kicked apart and bound to the apparatus. He took my limp arms and buckled them high and stretched further than they should be. The strain finally kicked my brain into gear.

"Aren't you supposed to ask permission to touch?"

"You've been bad. Bad girls get punished."

"What about my safe word?"

His answer to that was ripping my dress from my body, exposing my back. I let out a yell. This was not what I wanted. I didn't know what I expected, but this wasn't it. Emotions finally returned to me along with a good dose of fear. *What the hell am I doing here?*

"I like screaming. Bad girls don't get a safe word."

Panic rose in me as I pulled against the restraints. There was no give to them. This was not the same as giving up control to someone else. This was not the same at all. No trust existed in this scene. When Conspiciens dominated our encounters, I still had a choice. His ministrations had always been firm and pushed my limits, but he never went so far as to scare me. I had my safe word and never had to use it with him. This man, whoever he was, took away any say I had and the thought being forced terrified me beyond anything I'd ever experienced. "Please, I don't want this anymore. I don't know what I'm doing. Please stop."

"I like begging too."

Oh God, this man was going to hurt me! I struggled harder, and my wrists started to bleed. "No, please let me go. I'm sorry. I shouldn't be here. I'm not in a good place right now and..."

"Bad girls get punished."

A swishing noise warned me just a millisecond before fire burst across my back as a full lash struck me. I screamed and pulled hard at the restraints, fighting like a cornered animal. "Please stop. Peaches! Peaches is my safe word!"

Another lash landed, bringing more pain. "I'm sorry, please, please, please, let me go!"

A third strike hit my back, and I cried out again. *Why did I do this? What drove me to come here? This wasn't me, yet I put myself in this position.* My mental gymnastics bounced around from thought to thought and finally settled on one. *I'm so fucked up. Maybe I do deserve this.*

Another hit and I jerked at the impact, this time with only a whimper. Bile rose in my throat, and the world started to fade. My frantic pulls against the cuffs relaxed as I took my punishment.

The door banged open, and I heard a scuffle and the sound of fists hitting flesh.

"Get him out of here before I kill him. Christ, look at her back."

"Fuck, how bad is it?"

"Cocksucker used a belt. Broke the skin in several places."

"Get her down and take care of her. I'll deal with the asshole. Take my keys. She can't ride your bike like that."

The painful pull on my wrists released, and I sagged into a pair of strong arms. My head rolled back to take in the face of my rescuer. Angus's green eyes looked back at me in a tight, grim face. "I'm getting you out of here and seeing to your back. Then you and I are going to have a talk, and you're going to tell me why the fuck you came here like this."

Fire danced over my body from the strained muscles and lashes, but gladness filled me as he took over. He might sound mad, but he would never hurt me. I had no doubts that I could trust Angus MacAteer with my life.

He wrapped me in a blanket and lifted me in his arms, taking care not to touch the parts of my back where the lashes landed. The moment he settled me in the warm cradle of his chest, a sense of relief overwhelmed both my mind and my body. Tears flowed freely as I buried my face in his neck.

"Easy, babe. I've got you. You want to go to the hospital?"

Humiliation. Admitting to strangers where I'd been and what I'd done. Paperwork, and the possibility of it getting back to my parents. I stiffly shook my head. "Please, don't."

His sigh told me he didn't like my answer, but he'd abide by it. "Alright for now, sweetheart, but I reserve the right to take you later if I think it's necessary. Understand?"

I had no idea where he took me, but the car stopped sooner than I expected. He carried me into a squat cabin-like place that resembled a shack more than a house.

"My plan was to find a different place, but since Patrick moved in with Sloane, I decided to stay on here for a while until I found what I wanted. Thought about finding a piece of land and building my own house. This one is a right dump, but clean and okay enough for a temporary place to live."

He set me down in one of the bedrooms, and I carefully rolled to my stomach. My back, buttocks, and thighs throbbed painfully, and I had the urge to beat my head against something hard.

Why did I do this to myself?

"Here, take these. They're an anti-inflammatory

and a muscle relaxer to help with the pain. I'm gonna clean the cuts and put some oil on your back. Might sting a bit at first, but it will make you feel better."

Air hissed through my teeth as he dabbed at the cuts. A moment later his cool breath soothed the burn. I stayed still and let him take care of me. His calm and tender ministrations made me want to cry, and a whimper escaped my lips.

"I know, sweetheart. Almost done."

A pleasant scent came to my nostrils as he smoothed oil over my abused skin. I sniffed. "What's in it?"

"Aloe gel with helichrysum, frankincense, and lavender oils. Supposed to help with blood flow and bruising."

"Oh." My voice sounded watery and weak to me, so I stopped talking and concentrated on Angus's gentle fingers. Gradually, the pain faded. Angus had come to my rescue again and taken care of me. But why was he at the club? And how did he know what was happening to me? Facts aligned themselves. The motorcycle, the biker gloves, the commanding air Angus always seemed to exude and that exact same manner from the man I knew at the club.

"You're Conspiciens, aren't you?" I said this question very matter-of-factly.

His slick fingers stopped their glide over my back and thighs for a moment, then resumed their soothing motions. "I planned on telling you this week when we had our talk. I've been racking my brain for the best way of breaking the news. I hope you're not mad about it."

"I suppose I could be, but I'm not. It's more like relieved that I'm not going crazy over two men. That probably didn't come out right, but it's been a shit-storm of a day and I have no idea what to think or feel or do."

"Is that why Rhyleigh showed up at the club and not Tacet?"

A shard of shame pierced my heart. "I'm not sure who showed up at the club."

"Look at me, Rhyleigh."

I raised my head and met his gaze. He sat on the floor next to the bed, so we were eye to eye. Those green orbs held me in thrall. "I think you can guess that I have secrets, too, that very few people know. No one in my family knows this side of me, and only one other person besides you has my club and real names. If you can't guess, that's Cory the manager of the Donjon."

I shifted and my bare nipples brushed against the quilt on the bed. "What happened to my clothes?"

"Ruined when that bastard ripped them off you.

No big loss as that dress was ugly as hell. I have some stuff you can wear. You hungry?"

I smiled at his obvious attempt at changing the subject to something more normal. It made my stomach gurgle in response and he chuffed at the noise. "I have some leftover Irish stew and biscuits. I'll go heat it up. We'll eat and give ourselves a little time, then we're going to talk. Can you sit at the table, or do you want me to bring it here?"

"I'll come sit. I'd rather not spill food on your bed."

His eyes shone with humor. "We're not talking about five-star accommodations, sweetheart. A few crumbs aren't a big deal. That's why those little hand vacs are so cool."

I wanted to cry at his gentle compassion. I couldn't remember a time in my life when anyone had shown this kind of care for me.

He grinned and kissed my temple as he helped me up and into the kitchen. I marveled that even when I leaned on him hard, he took my weight and didn't let me fall. We ate on the coffee table in front of the couch as he didn't have a furnished dining area.

"This is really good. I had no idea you could cook."

He shrugged and tore off a piece of bread. "I've

learned enough to feed myself, but that's about it. You?"

"About the same."

Dusk had fallen across the sky and I could see the colors through the window. A blend of gray, periwinkle, pink, and peach floated above the mountain backdrop. Angus picked up the bowls and took them into the sink. When he came back, he moved me to sit across his lap and folded his arms around me in a cocoon. The pain in my back had dulled, but he was careful where he touched me. My head fit naturally in the spot between his shoulder and neck, and I let out a contented sigh.

"You hear that?"

I listened in concentration, but only a faint chorus of tree frogs and katydids caught my ears. "I don't hear anything."

"See anyone here besides me?

"No. We're alone."

He flexed his arms. "Feel that?"

"Yes. Feels good."

"I meant what I said. You're safe with me. There are four walls that I promise will not judge you or hurt you, and nothing you say will go beyond this house. Now you're going to talk to me."

His tone sounded gentle but underneath I heard the order. My nerves jumped, but the sheer panic I experienced earlier today didn't come back. Instead, it was more towards relief. "I don't know where to begin."

"Start with whatever is in the front of your mind and work your way through."

His clean scent and low tone surrounded me. He was right. I felt safe with him. Safer than I had in a long time.

"I was the unplanned child that just happened to come along at the wrong time. My sister is five years older than me and supposed to be the only one. Mom used to call me 'her little mistake' while I was growing up." I snorted without humor at the thoughtless reminder Mom gave me regularly. "I really wasn't abused or neglected, I guess, but I always considered myself as the afterthought. Deidre always came first. If she had a dance recital and I had a game at the same time, my parents went to her event. Today was no different. She had a fancy art charity party for her work and my mom insisted I go. I think she bought me that hideous dress to make sure I didn't take any attention from Deidre."

He gave a short laugh against my ear. "I agree on the dress."

I relaxed a little more at the comforting sound of his laugh and took strength from his embrace to continue. "I heard some ladies talking about me in the bathroom, saying stuff about how many problems Deidre's sister had. Can't hold a job. Didn't make it in college. Still lives at home. It got to me to hear someone list my faults like that. To top it off, I met Deidre's boyfriend for the first time. I knew him when he dated a friend of mine. He…"

My breath hitched, and I had to stop speaking as my throat closed up. Angus waited patiently for me to get it together.

"You have to know that neither my mom nor my dad talked to me about sex. Ever. I didn't know about periods until I had one when I turned thirteen. I started bleeding at school and had really bad cramps. It terrified me 'cause I had no idea what it was, and I thought I was dying of cancer or something. The gym coach took me aside, and he explained it all to me. He even showed me how to use pads and tampons. I guess he should have got a female coach, but no one else was around and he took pity on me and my ignorance. I told my mom what happened, and she just shrugged and walked away."

Angus made a humming noise. "So a male coach taught you about your body."

I nodded. "Yes. He didn't make fun of me or make me feel embarrassed or stupid. I think he saw how scared I was and simply took care of me. I joined his volleyball team later and became one of his star players."

"How does that relate to today?"

I swallowed. "I got my sex education the same way. The semester after my period came, a big group of us had to take a one-day class about it in school. They showed a cartoon anatomy drawing of a man and a woman. Penis, testicles, vaginas, ovaries, we learned all the parts, but not much more than that. Some girls talked about fucking in the locker rooms and how much they liked it, but dummy me couldn't quite figure out how everything worked."

Angus pressed a kiss against my forehead. "That's pretty rough. Especially during such a confusing time in life."

I hummed an agreement and continued. "I saw my first Shibari show in Atlanta when the volleyball team traveled there for a tournament. My best friend stole some tickets, and I saw Mr. and Mrs. Johnson for the first time. It scared the hell out of me seeing all the people in the strange gear and what they were doing, but then the Johnsons came to the stage."

A tear trickled down my cheek and I let it go. "It was the most beautiful thing I'd ever seen. They were so loving with each other. The level of devotion she had for him and the care he took with her... I'd never dreamed that love could be so extreme. I wanted that for me. Someone to love and care for me so deeply I could give it all to them and not be worried they would hurt me."

I sniffed as he squeezed me in a silent hug. "After high school, I tried college, not for any reason other than to get out of my parents' house. It didn't work too well, as I had no direction or purpose. I dropped out and moved in with a bunch of other girls in a house close to campus. Even though it was a tough time, I enjoyed it and had a kind of sisterhood thing going on. My roommate had a boyfriend, Ken, who started coming around and spending the night. He talked to me and made me laugh. I liked him a lot. He reminded me a little of my coach in that he didn't treat me like I was stupid. I thought he was nice. One night when I camped out on the couch, he came to me while everyone else slept."

I brushed away another tear and took one big, cleansing breath. "He gave me my first orgasm. I panicked a little when he put his mouth down there, but it felt so good I didn't stop him. When I came, it was huge, unexpected, and wonderful. So unbelievably wonderful that I fell in love with him. At that point, I'd do anything he wanted me to do. When he spread my legs and pushed inside me, I stayed quiet even though it hurt like hell. After he finished, he kissed me and went back to Gemma. I had a lot of mess to clean up from me and the couch so my room-mates wouldn't know."

My heart clenched with regret, and I pressed into Angus's body harder. "Whatever he told me to do that night, I did. He told me to suck his penis. He told me to get on all fours so he could fuck me from behind. Everything he wanted from me, I did without question or protest, *and I liked it.*"

Angus's breathing got noticeably deeper. "Is that when you discovered you were a sub?"

"Probably, although I couldn't put a name to it. I didn't know anything about anything. I was with Ken for only the one night, but it changed my world. I really thought he loved me and he simply waited for the right time to tell Gemma. I was so damn stupid. Work let me off early one afternoon, and I found them in bed together. She didn't say anything about he and I having sex, but I heard her complain to him about all the attention he gave me. I can still remember the knife to my heart when he told her he found my little crush on him amusing."

My voice broke and faded as more tears fell. "I couldn't afford a place of my own, and I didn't want roommates in case I might fall into the same trap. My mom offered for me to move back in as she thought it a humiliation to have her daughter live the way I lived. I've been there ever since. Still an embarrassment. Still a failure."

Angus shifted me on his lap. "Did he use a condom?"

I shook my head. "I never asked him. Thankfully, I didn't get pregnant or catch anything."

"You shouldn't have had to ask, but that's another long conversation. Still doesn't tell me what happened today that drove you into the club, sweetheart."

"I found out Ken is my sister's new boyfriend and my possible brother-in-law. He was at the party, and he recognized me. I had no idea how to handle it."

I gave a little laugh. Angus didn't. "He thought it would be a treat to do two sisters in one day. He started to…."

Angus's arms tightened around me. "Did he touch you?"

"No, I got away. Then I heard both my mom and Deidre talking about me. About how much of a failure I am and how I've been nothing but a burden my whole life. It meant nothing to them how I've worked at becoming a yoga instructor and co-owning a business. I'm worthless in their eyes and always will be."

I openly cried now, not caring if the remnants of my makeup streaked. "I think I went to the club because I needed to feel something. Anything other than a useless empty shell. I didn't plan on getting whipped, and I've never been interested in that side of it, but when that man ordered me to follow him, I didn't think about it. I just did it."

Shame flowed over me as I cried, clutching Angus's shirt and soaking us both. "Why am I like this? I'm supposed to be a strong, independent woman who can stand up for herself with a no-nonsense attitude and take no bullshit from anyone. Instead, I'm this insignificant person who would rather be dominated and told what to do."

He rocked me lightly and crooned in my ear. "Hush now, darlin'. I got you."

After I'd emptied myself, I got the hiccups. He didn't laugh or tease me about it. He waited until they subsided. "There's a lot to unpack here, sweetheart, and I think you've had enough tonight. We're gonna talk some more tomorrow after I take care of your back again. I have a lot of thoughts, and one of them is finding this Ken fellow and throat-punching that son-of-a-bitch, then cussing your family."

He moved me so I straddled his lap. I flushed at the sight I must present, but he put a finger under my chin so I had to raise my face to him and meet his eyes. "Some things I'm going to tell you now, though, and you're gonna listen. First, it's clear you need a

Dom of some form, and that's me. I promise I'll take care of you without pain or humiliation or force. That's not what it's about and you need someone safe to explore with. Second, you are not going back to live with your parents after tonight. You're staying here with me. When you go get your stuff, I'll be there with you. I'm not going to let you face them alone."

My heart zinged at his words. Both for his declaration to be my Dom, and support with my family, and it thrilled even more at his next words.

He cupped my cheeks in his hands and gazed at me with an intensity that took my breath away. "Third, you are not worthless. Did you hear me? You. Are. Not. Worthless. And it pisses me the hell off that anyone would ever make you feel that way. So what if you didn't go to college? I barely graduated high school, yet I'm well known and respected in my field. You have a gift for helping people. I remember how you lit up when you told me about one of your yoga ladies reaching her fitness goals. Pure fucking joy at someone's triumph in your class. You were so beautiful. I think that's when I started falling for you."

Falling for me?

"How's your back?"

"It's… um… okay."

"Good. Now you're going to go into the bathroom

and get ready for bed. There's a pack of new tooth-brushes in the cupboard. You can use my comb and soap and stuff. I'll get you one of my T-shirts to wear, and you'll sleep with me from now on. Understand?"

Anticipation started fluttering in my lower half. I nodded.

"Say it out loud, sweetheart."

"I understand."

He leaned in for a soft, gentle kiss. "Excellent. Now go wash your face, babe. I'll be in the bedroom waiting for you."

I did as I was told. The soap he had smelled fresh and masculine. I pumped a palmful of hand lotion from the dispenser next to the sink and moisturized my face. Drug store brand and far from designer, but I didn't care. I regarded my reflection in the mirror. Same face as yesterday, but something seemed differ-ent. My eyes might be just a tad brighter now, my mouth a little poutier, and my brows soft and relaxed instead of pinched up with stress.

"He loves me, flaws and all." I told my image. No, that wasn't right. He didn't see my craving to be dominated as weird or bad. He didn't see me as weak or less. He didn't see me as a failure or a burden or awkward or embarrassing or any of those things that my family saw. I watched as tears filled my eyes. It was overwhelming and scary and wonderful and so much more that I could hardly contain the emotions welling up in me. All my life, I'd been programmed to doubt myself, and those doubts were still there, but now through Angus's eyes I saw a new Rhyleigh with great potential and hope to become who she's supposed to be. I stood up straight and wiped the wet from my eyes and cheeks. My chin came up, and I smiled. My reflection smiled back.

CHAPTER TEN

The confrontation with my mom went about how I expected.

"How dare you leave the party like that? Outrageous! You embarrassed your sister to death in front of her boss. Such horrible manners. What were you thinking?"

"I told you I felt sick."

"That's no excuse for your deplorable behavior."

Her barbs had no impact. Normally, they tore me to shreds in a few seconds, but today, they had no effect on me. It had to be Angus's presence at my back. "You won't have to worry about that anymore. I'm moving out."

The look on her face went from indignant to furious. "You did this before and it was a disaster. A complete disregard of your father and I, living in that… that… squatter's house."

"I paid my way."

"Working jobs that are beneath the family dignity. You've always been trouble and the way you've held your sister back? It's disgraceful. You will stay here and behave yourself as befits your station and not make any more trouble."

Angus spoke behind me, and steel entered my spine. "No, she's not."

Mother jerked back at his words. "Who are you and why do you think you have a say so?"

"I'm Angus and I'm Rhyleigh's man."

Rhyleigh's man. I loved hearing those words!

Mother sneered and didn't bother to answer him. She turned to me as I finished packing up my trophies and picture scrapbooks. "Not one penny. You understand me? You won't get an ounce of help from me or your father. If you dare walk out of this house, it will be for the last time. Cut off completely."

I didn't know how to react to my mother's announcement, but Angus did. He laughed. He actually laughed at my mom. "That's not a problem. She doesn't need your money when she has me."

"Oh? Are you independently wealthy? You certainly don't look like it."

Angus shrugged as he lifted a box of my stuff on

his shoulder. "I'm not a millionaire, but I make a nice six figures a year and have some heavy investments for the future. She won't go without."

Mother showed surprise that anyone would contradict her. "I'm sure that won't last. She'll drain you dry like she has her father and me. She'll..."

"Monique, give it a rest."

My father suddenly appeared, and my mother's mouth snapped shut. "Is this what you want, Rhyleigh?"

A lump rose in my throat. "Yes, Dad."

He gave a decisive nod. "Go be happy."

He walked out. I think that was the first time I'd ever seen my mother speechless.

Angus excused himself to take the box he carried to the truck. Four more and two large suitcases later, I drove away following Angus's truck. I should have been sadder to leave, but I'd cried myself out already and had nothing left to grieve. Perhaps more emotion would come at some point. Right now numbness fit the best description of my attitude.

Once we got to the house, he moved my boxes into the second bedroom and my suitcases into his room. "Take whatever space you need, babe. Jodie is covering your classes for a few days, right?"

"Yes, she is."

"I took the day off today, but I'll have to work

some extra hours the rest of the week. Owen's got four big jobs, and Connor has two sheds and a kitchen cabinet job. Gonna be all hands on deck to get them done."

"Oh, no, Angus. You don't have to put yourself out over me."

He moved to the large dresser and started rearranging drawers to make room for my stuff.

"You haven't figured it out yet, have you, sweetheart? You're my woman now. You belong to me and that means you joined the MacAteer clan. Owen's baby had an ear infection a few weeks ago, and he missed some days to be with Melanie. We took up the slack so he could take care of his family. Connor's furniture business has skyrocketed. Garrett spent extra time helping him prep new wood for turning and did some varnishing to help him catch up. Bertie had that nasty shit with her ex-husband, and we came together as a family to help her get through it. Patrick is thinking about making a new path for himself as a bartender at Gallaghers's. He and Sloane have decided to do some renovations to the building and put in a restaurant along with the pub. That's a big job, and we'll be ready to do it for them when the time comes, and at cost to keep their opening expenses down. I called Owen last night and told him you had some bad family trouble and needed my help. He told me to take whatever time you needed. No questions and no arguments."

No one had ever gone out of their way to help me and care for me like Angus had. The idea that his whole family had my back stunned me into silence. He came to me and took me in his arms. "Chin up, sweetheart. That's what the MacAteer men are like. It's not only me you have in your corner. You have all of us behind you. Connor, Beverly, Owen, Melanie, Garrett, Bertie, Patrick, Sloane, and me. One hundred percent with no expectations."

I had no words to identify the emotions that welled up inside me. "That's so… I can't…."

He smiled and lightly kissed me. "You'll get used to it."

"But we haven't… um… you and me never…."

"Had sex? Not in the conventional sense, but I don't have to put my dick inside you to know your body intimately and stake my claim. We'll get to that when you're ready. I think your back needs a few more days. I can wait."

"But what if I can't?" *Who was this flirty woman? Another Rhyleigh?*

He threw back his head and laughed. "Oh, darlin', you're killing me. I'd like nothing better than to strip you out of those clothes and bury myself inside you, but I have no desire to hurt you, and you've had enough change thrown your way."

One finger stroked down my cheek under my chin, and he lifted my mouth to hover under his. "When I take you, I'm going to be absolutely thorough, and there will be no doubt you're mine, and I'm yours. I need to set up some things to make that happen. I can do vanilla if you prefer for our first time, but we both like a dash of spice, so I thought I'd make it a night of exploration for both of us."

A series of sun flares started low in my belly. "That sounds great."

"Good." He moved away with a big grin, deliberately leaving me hanging. "Which side of the bed do you want?"

The numbness I thought filled me wasn't right either. I did feel numb, but as I looked into Angus's earnest face, a small bit of something open in my chest. A seed. One that would grow as long as I nourished it. Hope.

LATER THAT NIGHT, ANGUS MADE A LOW COUNTRY BOIL for dinner, a simple one-pot recipe with shrimp, pieces of kielbasa, corn on the cob, red potatoes, and Old Bay seasoning. We sat on the couch side by side while semi-watching a movie and eating. I say semi because we kept talking instead of paying attention to the screen. I asked him loads of questions, and he patiently answered them.

"I noticed you were Angus instead of Conspiciens at the club. Why?"

"A Shibari show is coming up, and the owner had me inspect the rigging." He picked up another shrimp and tossed it in his mouth. "I designed and built it for them, so I know what to look for and to keep everything safe.

"Really?"

He grinned. "Yeah, sweetheart. I used to goof around a lot on job sites and not pay much attention to regulations. I messed around too much one afternoon, and my younger sister paid the price. The safety harness was faulty, and I kept teasing her until it slipped. She fell off a roof and broke her leg. She could have died, and it would have been my fault. Safety is important for anyone practicing Shibari or anything else at the club."

"How did you know I needed help?"

"The hallways have cameras, and I happened to be with Cory in the view room when that asshole took you. The private rooms don't have cameras in them, but they do have audio. Anyone using a private room has to obtain verbal permission and a stated safe word. Staff monitor the rooms and check the audio for problems. If someone doesn't give permission, or shouts a safety word and it is not honored, they go in and take care of the problem. Gave me a fucking heart attack when I heard you screaming "peaches" over and over again."

"Would you have stopped it, anyway?"

He scooped up a piece of kielbasa. "I was on my way to the room when you started screaming. I knew something was wrong when you showed up as Rhyleigh and not Tacet, but even if you had come in as that persona, I still would have stopped it. Breaking the rules or not, no way would I have let you stay with that guy. He gave off too many bad vibes. Cory has banned his ass from the club. Fucker has no clue what being a Dom is."

I leaned back on the sofa and stretched. My back barely twinged. His oil concoction worked wonders. "How did you get into this stuff?"

He wiped his mouth with a napkin and leaned back to join me. "My life is not unlike yours in some ways. All I've known since childhood was work and family. My Da said jump and all of us did it. I didn't have the abuse you did, but I didn't have any control either. My twin is the more outgoing between us, and I love him for that, but I've also spent time in his shadow. That's not a complaint; that's just how it is.

We used to do a lot of partying and I've been with my share of women. Lots of one-nighters or one-weekers." He barked a short laugh. "It's a miracle we never caught anything."

I cringed a little at his words. He had a lot more sexual experience than I did, but how much of that included any kind of relationship? Not a lot from the way he told his history. Had he ever told any other woman he fell for them? My gut instinct was he had not.

He grew pensive as he spoke. "Anyway, we had a job contract for a few months in Maryland and I met Zinnia. At least, that was the name she used. The first night I met her, she introduced me to Shibari. She took me to a club, tied me up, and spent hours giving and taking pleasure. I've been hooked ever since. I think the appeal is twofold. I get to have total control, and it's something that's mine I don't have to share with my siblings. It's a part of me that's private and I like having that little bit of separation. I love my family, but I need my life to be mine. Make sense?"

I nodded and dropped my head to his lap. "I get that. My parents, especially my mom, tried for years to make me fit a mold that wasn't made for me. It's a hard position to maintain."

He moved his arm to make room and draped it

lightly over my shoulders, being mindful of my back. "Yeah, it is."

"So, did you get into… um… other stuff?"

He laughed again. "You mean flogging, spanking… that sort of thing? Not really. I tried, but I didn't like it. It doesn't do anything for me to hit a woman, no matter what the situation. Zinnia asked me to paddle her, and it seemed wrong. You into any of that?"

I snuggled into his thigh and sighed. "Not really. I saw a lot of stuff at the club that looked extreme and painful. There were some things I wanted to try, but I… well… I was ashamed for having the desire to be tied up, let alone other stuff. I've thought of myself as a sick freak for years." I shook my head and laughed. "I can't believe I said that out loud."

"Feels good to share, doesn't it?"

I smiled up at him. "Yes, it does."

It did feel good. Like Shibari knots untying in my stomach and I could truly breathe free for the first time.

His fingers stroked through my hair and massaged my scalp. "There's nothing to be ashamed about, babe. If something feels good to you, I don't see any reason you have to suppress it or think of it as bad. Trust is the key. Partners need to have the absolute most confidence in each other that they are safe and their needs will be met, but it will take time and communication and care to get there. You've accepted me as your Dom, and that means we'll share what we like, what we don't like, things we want to try. There's a lot of mutual respect between a Dom and a sub. You've seen how it can be with the Johnsons. That's an unbreakable bond of love, and that's what it's all about. I'm really hoping you and I can have that when we're ready for it."

The last few days took their toll on me and my eyes grew heavy. The safe environment and warmth of his body made me sleepy. "I do trust you, Angus. You make me feel beautiful and normal."

"You are normal, sweetheart. I'll keep repeating that until you understand it."

"It might take a long time."

"I'm a patient man. I'll be here."

CHAPTER ELEVEN

The family cookout had been outstanding over at
Bertie's Mountainside Inn. I'd been living with
Angus for about a week when the invitation came for
a spur-of-the-moment food fest. We showed up with
a lemon cake we picked up at a local bakery. Angus
held my hand and led me to where everyone gath-
ered at the picnic shelter behind the main building.
Sticky summer heat meant I wore shorts and a
sleeveless shirt, with my hair braided into a ponytail.
Angus had his hair twisted into a long braid for the
afternoon. I'd binged watched the first season of The
Vikings on Netflix not too long ago. Ragnar Lothbrok
had nothing on my man.

"It's different," I remarked as we got on his
motorcycle to ride back.

"What, babe?" He handed me a full helmet.

"Before, I was just Rhyleigh, yoga person. Now I'm Rhyleigh, Angus's woman. No one blinked an eye or said anything, and I got folded into the mix. No muss, no fuss."

He grinned at me as he flipped his finger for me to raise my head. His fingers checked the helmet's chin strap. "Told you so. It only gets better from here."

I took a cleansing breath to ask the question that had brewed in my mind for several days. "I saw the pulleys and hooks you installed in the second bedroom. Are we going to make it better soon?"

His eyes glittered before as he lifted his own helmet to his head. "Tonight, if that's what you want."

The time had arrived, and a giddiness waved through my head. *Who was this bold vixen? I like her!* "I want."

"Then you'll get."

On the ride back to the house, nervous flutters and starbursts competed in my body. Seated behind Angus with my crotch pressed into his behind and my arms wrapped around his middle, I sensed every move. He'd shift gears and the vibrations of the big machine made me quiver with need.

When we got to the house, he told me to dismount and go inside while he put the bike away.

Butterflies tickled my middle as I went directly into the bedroom to wait for him.

My gaze turned upward to the rigging he'd built. I knew it would be sturdy and safe.

Safe. A word with many nuances, one of them being trust. This would be a turning point for me. Life-changing. At one time, I would not have considered taking this step, being too scared or guilty about it to try.

A big grin burst across my face. Now, I couldn't wait.

Angus came into the room. His eyes met mine and the green darkened. He carried a box of coiled silk ropes and some other supplies. His name might be Angus, but I clearly saw Conspiciens in front of me. "Take off your clothes."

I stripped off my shirt and dropped my shorts in quick, efficient movements. My body was shaking with too much adrenaline for a seductive striptease. Bra and panties followed, and I kicked everything to the side. I'd shaved earlier in preparation and my pussy itched some from the loss of hair. Its bareness made me feel more naked, but then Angus gave me his approval with his pointed scrutiny. "Stand in ready position. You know what that is?"

I preened at little, growing more confident in my role. "Yes." I folded my arms behind my back and placed my feet a shoulder-width apart. Anticipation made me hyperaware of everything around me.

I watched as he took off his own clothes, and my mouth watered at the strong body he revealed. Wide shoulders, defined arms, and a set of tight washboard abs, all of this belonged to me, and I imagined his taste as I explored those lines with my tongue. The real shock came when I spotted his piercings. Three barbells decorated the length of his heavy penis, and another showed completely through from top to bottom behind the broad head. My mouth watered as he pulled a ring from the box and fastened it around the base of his hard dick under his ball sack.

"The cock ring will make me last longer, and I have every intention of making this go as long as possible."

He donned a robe, dimmed the lights, and lit a few candles. The scent of sandalwood, along with soft ethereal instrumental music, floated in the background. He set the stage so all my senses engaged for the coming experience.

All the while, Angus remained relaxed and quiet. He moved in front of me after he finished his preparations, and his face broke into a tender smile. "Permission to touch?"

I smiled back. "Yes."

"Safe word?"

"Peaches."

He lowered his head to mine and gave me a long, loving kiss. I kissed him back, touching his lips lightly with my tongue. After all the Shibari shows I watched, being a part of this private one highlighted everything in me. I couldn't wait any longer.

We began.

He loaded the pockets of his kimono with stuff from the box so he wouldn't have to interrupt the flow. He moved behind me and started winding the first rope around my shoulders and chest. It was tight but not uncomfortable. He left my breasts exposed as each layer encircled me. He gently bound my arms behind me. I felt each wrap contain my movements and restrict my control. It didn't hurt as more coils were added, but the sense of helplessness grew, thrilling me.

His hands came around and cupped each breast as he kissed my neck. "Okay, babe?"

Was I? I swallowed and tested the tightness and comfort of the ropes. "Yes."

He picked up a water bottle and gave me a drink before continuing his tying. Chest, ribs, shoulders, arms, hips, knees, legs, he cocooned every inch of my body in intricate knots. He kissed each part before adding another rope. Diamond-shaped ladders covered my stomach. Rope squares crisscrossed on my thighs and calves. Other ropes tied into the knots and hung loosely from the rigging. My belly quivered as he tugged and tightened. At last he stepped back, his hands on the braided ropes hanging overhead. His green eyes glowed with desire as he looked at my body covered in his art. I felt beautiful.

"Ready?"

"Yes." My voice was throaty and low. "Please."

He pulled down and my weight dropped back into the intricate harness he tied around me. It was an even bigger loss of control as my feet left the ground. The ropes bit into my skin as he hoisted me in the air in a gentle arch with my breasts pushed out. He paused to let me catch my breath.

"Okay?"

"Yes." My heartbeat increased as my senses opened more.

He lifted one breast to his mouth and sucked the nipple into a point. I cried out at the electric bolt that shot straight through me. He spent several minutes leisurely playing with my breasts, tracing them with his tongue. When the sensation got too much with one, he'd switch sides, knowing my body better than I knew it myself. I writhed in the rigging, but I had no control except to let him do what he wanted.

Noises of both want and frustration came from my throat.

He wove another rope through the windings on my knees and legs. The next pull over the rigging brought my legs up, settling me into a cradle that put me nearly horizontal to the ground with my legs high and spread wide. I gasped at the sudden display of my core to the cool air. My head fell back into a rope nest and my eyes glued to the man who stepped between my thighs. There was nothing I could do but hang here.

His hands moved over the ropes covering my body. "Anything too tight or digging into your skin so bad you can't take it for a long period of time?"

It was Conspiciens growl I heard. I couldn't believe I didn't make the connection earlier. "No, the balance is perfect. Please don't stop."

I didn't have the words to tell him what I experienced. Nothing could describe it except I wanted more. His hands drifted over my breasts and ribs to my buttocks. I could feel his gaze on my most hidden parts.

"I'm going to plug your ass now, same way as before. This will get you ready for me to take it later. Are you good with that?"

My mouth watered, and I swallowed. "Yes."

"Keep your eyes on mine."

My gaze locked with his. I couldn't look away even if I wanted to.

He reached into his pocket and I heard the snick of a cap. I jumped a little as his fingers touched between my open buttocks, spreading the cold gel on my ass. One pressed against my tight ring and pushed at it until I relaxed enough to let him enter. A moan spilled out of me at the intimate intrusion. He worked the finger in and out up to the second knuckle and added a second, making the burn more intense.

"Breathe, Rhyleigh. Breathe deep through your nose and out of your mouth, just like in your classes."

I did as he instructed and he eased in three fingers. A cry escaped at the sensation. It wasn't painful, but it did push the boundaries.

"Okay, baby?"

"More. I need more." *Who was this person?* I didn't know myself anymore.

His fingers slid out of my slick ass and he reached into his pocket. More gel spread across my ring and I felt the hard tip of the plug. He pushed the cone in and out, stretching me further.

"Push out, sweetheart." I bit my lip as he worked the plug into my ass, twisting and turning until it was fully seated. His fingers glided over my pussy to test my readiness. I knew I was dripping wet, and he spread the slickness over my twitching clit, pinching and rolling it.

The mew that came from my mouth was full of longing need. Fire blazed up as he played.

I wanted to come. I *needed* to come.

"Please," I begged.

"Not yet."

He bent over and flicked his tongue against my distended clit. My mews turned into gasps. Fire raced to my head and my muscles spasmed.

"Angus, I need to come!"

"Wait for it, Rhyleigh. Hold back."

I fought against the ropes, not trying to escape from them, but from the urge to move. My ass burned around the plug as my pussy contracted with the desire to be filled. The need to come was so intense I started crying.

His head came up, and I panted to slow my heart rate. He tore open a condom packet with his teeth and smoothed the thin latex over his erection. It barely fit him. He took himself in his hand and brushed the hard, pierced tip over my opening, coating himself in my wetness.

"Look at me, Rhyleigh."

I stopped twitching and locked eyes with him again. The fierceness of his gaze held me in place as the head parted my folds and entered. My mouth dropped open. He pressed slowly forward, feeding each inch inside. My channel clenched around him as it stretched to accept his length. He withdrew a little and pressed in further, gradually working himself in until he was all the way seated.

Tears fell from my eyes at the intense connection. My body was full, so full of sensation. My head, my ass, my breasts, my clit, my pussy, everything in me pulsed with an awareness nothing in my life had ever matched. I felt his breathing, the blood flowing in his veins, the pleasure in his body, the care he had for me, and the pure joy of at last being inside me.

"Angus!"

"Yeah, love, I feel it too."

He withdrew from my body and thrust back in slowly, drawing out every drop of sensation with those little balls from his piercing caressing me. Stroke after stroke, he brought me closer to the edge until I thought I'd go insane from the need to climax.

He let me.

I closed my eyes as I convulsed in the harness of ropes, coming hard in my bondage. White light burst behind my lids, and my ears roared with ocean-like waves as a huge orgasm hit. I cried out with a level of pleasure I'd never had before. As the first orgasm abated, a second came, deeper and longer than the first, and I screamed Angus's name.

He twisted and pulled the plug from me, dropping it on the floor. It bounced and rolled under me as he left my channel. The cock ring followed.

"Give me your eyes, babe. Look here."

The head slipped down to press into my ring, and I opened to him. He fed his still hard dick into my ass as he had my pussy, slow and steady. I cried out at this invasion I thought once to be taboo, but now I reveled in. The intense intimacy overwhelmed me as he pushed fully inside, making me take him, making me accept him, making me love him.

He pulled a thin pink wand with a knob on the end from his pocket. His thumb flicked a switch, and a muted buzz came to my ears.

"Tell me if it's too much."

He stroked the vibrating knob over my swollen clit and started moving in and out of my ass. I thought I'd reached the highest point I could, but I soon found I was far from the pinnacle.

"Angus!" I cried out as the sensations in my body grew to a depth I never dreamed of experiencing.

"I got you, babe." His heavy gasping echoed mine. "Give it to me. Give it all to me."

I came so hard, I almost passed out. He answered with a long howl of satisfaction. He pulsed inside me as he rammed in one last time. The vibrator turned off and dropped to the floor. The sudden silence was only broken by our panting and throaty sighs of completion. The music had run out some time ago, which I hadn't noticed until now.

He slipped out of my body, breaking the physical connection, but I still keenly felt his presence all through my body. He disposed of the condom, undid the anchoring ropes, and lowered me to the padded floor.

"Breathe with me, babe. In. Out. In. Out."

My bindings were still in place as he curled next to me, his warm body in contrast with the cool mats. We laid there, both coming down from the powerful mutual experience. Tears kept flowing from my eyes as I struggled to match my breaths with his.

"Breathe with me, baby."

I didn't know how long we stayed on the floor. Eventually, Angus shifted his weight and sat up. His hands shook as he tugged at the ropes one by one, coiling them as he went. My thighs and hips were slowly freed from the wraps, loops, and knots. He helped me sit up and took off the rest of the bindings, gradually returning control of my body to me. When I stood on wobbly legs, he scooped me into his arms and carried me into the master bedroom.

"I'll go get a couple water bottles."

I watched his naked butt flex as he left to go into the kitchen. He was such a beautiful man.

The cold water went down easy, and I hadn't realized how much I needed it. He sucked down half his bottle before coming up for air.

"Thirsty much?" I smiled up at him as I laid back on the bed.

He smiled back. "Good thing I have a case in the fridge." He came down on top of me and gave me a long, thorough kiss. He spent some time tracing the marks left by the ropes, massaging any tight muscles, and fetching a warm washcloth to clean me. I'd never been so cherished. His care of me brought a sense of peace I didn't think possible. Along with that peace came an eagerness. I looked forward to what came next.

"I don't know about you, sweetheart, but I'm drained."

"Me too."

He crawled into bed and spooned me. Both of us were still naked as he matched the curve of my body skin to skin. "Sleep, babe. We have the entire day tomorrow before work on Monday."

I shivered at his whisper in my ear. "You have more surprises for me?"

His low chuckle accompanied a quick kiss on the back of my neck. "I have a toy box full."

CHAPTER TWELVE

ANGUS DID INDEED HAVE A TOY BOX FULL OF DELIGHTS. We spent our last day off in bed or in the playroom, exploring and trying whatever we wished. I woke up when he rolled me to my back and entered me in straight-up vanilla missionary. His piercings contacted my G-spot, and even in that basic position, I came. I couldn't remember a time in my life where I'd been happier or more content.

He drove me crazy from constant sucking and playing with my sensitive breasts.

He tied me face down in a different sort of rope cradle to take me from behind.

He ate me so many times I lost count of the orgasms.

He used several different vibrators on me, inside and out.

He took my pussy.

He took my ass.

He taught me some simple knots and let me tie him spread eagle to his bed. I learned his musky taste and where his sensitive spots were located.

He loved it when I mounted him and gave him a full view of me rubbing my clit as I drove down on his hard dick.

The only issue happened when he tried to use nipple clamps. I stood tall in a rigging with my hands tied, and arms wrapped overhead. He prepared me for the clamps by sucking each nipple into a long point, then setting the tiny alligator teeth on me. I might have been too sensitive at the time, but it hurt.

"Oh! Please get them off!"

He didn't make me ask a second time. He quickly released the tension and removed them without pulling and making it worse. Relief from the sharp pain was immediate and his mouth moved to sooth the sting.

"I'm sorry, Angus, it really hurt and I don't think I can take them."

He kissed me. "Don't ever be sorry, babe. If what you're doing doesn't bring pleasure, you shouldn't be doing it. I know some people get off on it, but it doesn't do anything for me to cause pain. More like the opposite. The biggest turn on for me is seeing you bound in my ropes and watching you come apart when my dick is inside you."

I melted at his words. It still amazed me how much he cared and I didn't plan on ever taking it for granted.

He hooked one of my legs over his arm and lifted it to his shoulder. "I love that you're this flexible. We need to sort birth control soon so I can go without condoms. Almost used up the entire box. You willing to take that on?"

He slid inside me and I couldn't help but gasp at the sensation. "I'll make an appointment as soon as I can."

"Good. I can't wait to feel all of you, with nothing between us." He then proceeded to give me my first standing orgasm.

We didn't just have copious amounts of sex. We talked about us, our families, and our expectations. The more we spoke, the more I saw a future with him in it.

We finally made it to the bed later that night to watch a Netflix movie, cuddled into each other, exhausted from a glorious day of exploration. My body was sore in places not used to being sore, but that only enhanced my sense of satisfaction. He had just clicked off the TV when I brought up the subject of finances. "I lived with my parents because I don't make enough money for rent on my own. I don't have a lot, but I'll do my best to pay my half."

He looked down on me in amusement. I was curled into his side in the bed, and neither of us had bothered to put on any clothes all day. "You won't be paying any rent, sweetheart. It's month to month anyway, so we can take our time. We can go look for a nice house in the suburbs, or if you're game, I'd like to take a serious look at building our own place a little further out of town on a private plot of land. I've always wanted to have a log cabin style house. What do you think?"

This turn was so not what I expected to hear. "I… ah… what?"

His fingers slid up and down my side as he turned to face me. "I'm thinking four bedrooms so there's plenty of room for our kids and a nice, finished basement with a bonus room just for us. Sound good to you?"

"A cabin sounds wonderful." Then his other words unscrambled in my brain. "Kids?" I squeaked. Angus's chuckled as if he enjoyed keeping me off balance and guessing.

"Yeah. At least two, but maybe three. I'd like one of each—boy and girl—but I'll be okay with what we have."

"We're going to have kids?" My eyes grew wider as I struggled to comprehend what was happening.

His hand moved over and lightly squeezed one globe of my bottom. "Absolutely. You're going to be a great mother. We'd get married first."

Married? Did I want that? Yes, but not quite yet. Kids? I pictured a little girl with Angus's green eyes shining up at me. My heart danced with joy, but my stomach flipped with trepidation. "Wait. You're going a little fast. I just moved in with you yesterday."

"Am I?"

"Yes."

"Okay, dearest. Let me lay it out for you."

He rolled me to my back and moved on top of me, falling naturally between my legs with a perfect fit. "I make plenty of money for the both of us. You want to contribute? I get that, but you can buy the groceries and stuff like bedsheets and decorations. As your yoga business grows, we'll talk about putting some of your money away for retirement and for the kids' college funds. With me so far?"

My head whirled as it tried to keep up. "I think so."

"Yes, we're going to get married. I'm not asking. I'm telling. It's not going to happen next week so relax about that. We'll take the time we need until you're ready and we have our house built. I'm a patient man, and I've waited a long time to find my perfect life partner. That deep, solid connection between two people that is so fucking rare, very few find it. The Johnsons did. You've seen it."

I had seen it. Light beamed from my heart and radiated outward. Angus was right. We did have that same bond I'd seen so many years ago and craved for myself. Our bond might be new, but it was solid and would only get stronger.

"We have more to learn about each other, but we'll have a lifetime together to figure it all out." His head lowered, and he kissed me tenderly. As he shifted his hips, the tip of his hard dick touched right at my entrance. "I'm out of condoms, babe, but I'm good with taking a chance if you are. Christ, when I think about you swelling up with my child inside you, I want to burst with love."

"You love me?" I scarcely dared to breathe.

When he slowly pushed inside, I lifted my hips to take him. His head lowered, and he gave me the tenderest of kisses. "Rhyleigh, I fell in love with you the night we met at Gallaghers's. The universe made you for me and me for you. Can you feel it?"

I did. I felt it. That unspeakable joy that only comes with pure love. He stroked inside me, worshiping me, touching me with reverence, filling me with his essence, and giving it all to me.

"I love you too, Angus MacAteer."

We came together in a slow burn, finishing our sex marathon day by making love. Of all the climaxes he'd given me, this one was the best by far.

CHAPTER THIRTEEN

"MY GOODNESS, RHYLEIGH, YOU'RE MOVING LIKE AN old woman with severe arthritis. Are you all right?" Jodie greeted me with concern as she entered the studio part of the store. Her Bluetooth winked from its position in her ear, and she continued her one-sided conversation as she went to pull a box of essential oils from the storage closet.

Ever since she discovered the convenience of hands-free communication, that little bud became permanently embedded in her skull. I winced as I moved into an extended side pose. I'd been with Angus just over a month, and last night, we'd celebrated with extreme enthusiasm.

I was sore as hell.

With the upcoming expansion of the studio, I spent more working hours there during the day and had to quit my job at Trader Joe's. The work was already in progress as banging, wrenching, and crashing sounds came from the unit next door. Treatments like facials, body wraps, massages, manicures, pedicures, and other services had been discussed as offerings. Jodie already hit me up to go to the massage and yoga school for full licensure. Beverly's oldest daughter, Abby, also planned to go there as she was graduating high school soon and, like me, didn't want to do the four-year degree.

Jodie tapped the device to hang up and put her hands on her hips. "Well, poop. Jerry can't leave to join me for lunch, after all. Apparently, Clint got in another barroom fight and got himself beat up. I'm so glad you never got involved with that creep. I should never have set you up with him."

This news made me think about the condition of Angus's knuckles when he came home from hanging with his twin late Friday night at the pub. His lower jaw sported a purplish bruise, and his knuckles were swollen and bloody. When I asked him about it, he just smiled. "Nothing bad, darlin'. Just revoking a club membership."

I moved to a frog pose, relishing the stretch in my quads and hip flexors. I'd been tied in a similar pose last night, suspended in the playroom while Angus had his mouth....

"Earth to Rhyleigh. Come in, Rhyleigh."

"Sorry, Jodie. Just daydreaming a bit. What's up?"

"Someone is here to see you."

"For the ten o'clock class? It's only nine."

She shook her head. "I don't think so. Shall I send him back or make him wait?"

Him?

I moved out of the pose and stood up, taking a few deep, circular breaths to prepare myself for the confrontation I expected to happen. The only man I thought would take the time to seek me out would be Ken, perhaps looking to continue what he started at the company party. Not a chance. I closed my eyes and thought of last night when the broad head of Angus's dick breached my opening. The acute memory was so vivid, I still felt him moving inside me in the present. Right now, Angus worked next door, but he had my back no matter what space we occupied.

I turned, ready to face down my sister's boyfriend, but that's not who stood in front of me.

My father's eyes wandered around the studio, taking in the stack of mats, the wall of mirrors, and the giant lotus mural. "I had no idea."

The sadness in his voice cut through my surprise. He fixed his gaze on me and smiled. "How are you, Rhyleigh?"

"I'm good. I'm really good."

He nodded and continued examining the room. "The house has been in an uproar since you left. Your mother has been on the rampage and repurposed your room into a storage place. Deidre is determined to marry this Ken fellow, and that's the one thing that is making your mother happy. Planning this huge wedding." He sighed and shook his head. "Something about that guy. He acts sweet but slimy at the same time. Like canned peaches."

I bit my lip at his comparison. The old Rhyleigh would have kept silent and not rocked the boat anymore that she was already doing. "He is slimy, Dad. Deidre would be better off without him."

He looked at me sharply and for once I met his gaze without backing down.

"I'll get my golfing buddy to look into him. He's a judge over at the courthouse and has better access to public records. He's also a terrible locker room gossiper. If there is a smidgeon of a scandal, Monique won't have to throw a tantrum. Deidre will drop him like a stone if there's any hint he'll mess with her career."

It was strange sharing a laugh with this man. I didn't remember ever doing it before. His eye once again took in the beautiful lotus flower on the wall. "You've done this much on your own."

"I'm going to school in the fall for massage therapy and my full yoga instructor certificate. I've found where I fit in, and it's great."

"It's very impressive. I don't know how much that means to you since I've let you down as a father. I should have been there for you more growing up."

I couldn't disagree with him. The old me might demure, but not the new me. "Yeah, you should have."

I turned to see Angus entering the studio. He came right over to me and got in between my father and me. I saw my dad take a step back and then give a little satisfied smile. "I see you're in good hands. I have to get back to campus, but if you're good with me taking a class or two with you, I'd like to come."

"Sure, Dad. Sign up anytime."

He turned to leave but paused at the doorway. "For the record, I'm proud of you, Rhyleigh."

I managed to hold on until he left, then I turned into Angus's arms and relished in the love and support he offered. "You okay, sweetheart?"

I sniffed a little, but not with sadness. "Yes, I'm good. I think I just met my Dad. The real one."

Connor stood back from the smoking grill and blinked at the fragrant but harsh smoke. He and Owen manned the grill on this holiday weekend that marked the end of summer and the start of fall. The kids chased each other and yelled in the afternoon air.

"Give it back!"

"I had it first."

"No, you didn't."

"Mom!"

Connor laughed and sipped at his sweating bottle of beer. He didn't have to check to know his wife was gritting her teeth. She sat at the picnic shelter with Melanie and Bertie. Melanie had a cold lemonade in her hand instead of a beer. His little Sarah sat with them, as her older sister was absent. Abby got a job at the frozen custard stand, in addition to working a little at the inn and had discovered the joys of having her own money to spend.

"You boys are soooo immature!" Sarah snarked at her quibbling brothers.

Connor smiled at the girl's frustration and flipped one long slab of ribs. Owen picked up one of two giant platters to carry the meat. He spotted Garrett nearby, tossing pebbles into the small lake with baby Ryan.

The weather was perfect. The sun shone brightly in the clear sky, keeping the air warm but not too hot. Next week, The Mountainside Inn officially opened for guests, but today, all the amenities were reserved for family. Garrett had pointed out to Bertie that Labor Day weekend would be a great time to open, but she insisted that this weekend was for the MacAteers.

All of them.

Connor loaded the ribs on two huge platters, and he and Owen carried them to the middle of the oblong table. Melanie took one look at the oozing meat and turned an interesting shade of green.

"'Scuse me," she clipped as she covered her mouth and ran for the boathouse bathroom.

Beverly huffed and looked at her husband. "I can't believe she's pregnant again already. If Owen has his way, they'll have their own baseball team. All boys."

"Owen needs at least one little girl," Connor stated as he leaned over to kiss his wife. "Every father needs to experience the joys of Disney princess nights."

Pal, Bertie's adopted dog, woofed as Garrett approached the shelter with baby Ryan in his arms. A loud coughing rumble caught Connor's ear, and he grinned as he recognized the sound. It got louder and louder until a motorcycle appeared, followed by an SUV minivan. The rider dismounted, took off the helmet, and shook out a mane full of deep ginger hair.

"Auntie Eva!" Sarah's exuberant cry rang out as the girl dashed to slam into the woman. The SUV discharged a large blond Viking and four little girls.

Connor's heart swelled with delight as he waved at his only sister and youngest sibling. Her husband, Stud, was a member of a motorcycle club called the Dragon Runners, not too far away in Bryson City. They met a number of years ago when the MacAteer family was hired to rebuild their bar called River's Edge Bar. Stud had been quite the ladies' man at one time, but his total devotion to Eva and their daughters was undeniable. Connor was happy his sister had found the love of her life.

"Can you give me a ride on your bike?" Connor knew that entreating tone well. He'd heard it every time Sarah wanted something.

Eva grinned at her niece. "Only if Mom says it's okay. If you want it now, you'll have to ask Uncle S. He needs a break from the girls, and the car drives him bananas. He drove it here but will ride back later."

The man in question lifted a cooler over his shoulder from the back as three blonde female heads joined Beverly's kids at the playground. The fourth he carried in his other arm and handed her off to her mother. He gave his niece a half-smile on his god-like handsome face that probably meant a bike ride was in her future. Conner knew that just like himself, Stud had no resistance. His daughters had him wrapped around their little fingers and it looked like his niece had that same privilege.

Eva joined the gathering group at the picnic shelter and helped unpack the coolers of other foods. Coleslaw, green salad, buns, and deviled eggs made a huge feast next to the rib platters. Owen returned carrying a stockpot of green beans, and Connor brought an industrial-sized aluminum pan of crispy tater tots.

"God bless this food. Now y'all, dig in."

Beverly slapped a hand over her heart and

surprise broke over her face. "Did I hear right? Did Connor MacAteer utter the word 'y'all'?"

He looked at his wife and gave her a long raspberry. "Melanie's right. You are a PITA sometimes."

"Just for you, sweetheart, and you love me anyway."

Connor's face softened. "That I do."

The kids descended on the food like it was their last time to eat this summer. Bertie took a huge bite of a rib and let out a loud moan. "Oh, Connor, this is soooo good. I should hire you to cook this next weekend during the opening. People will come just for the food."

Connor grinned and threw an arm around Beverly. "My grill, but her recipe. We make a winning team, eh, Bev?"

She wiped a smear of sauce from her chin. "I should say something smart-aleck, but I don't have a thing. Yes, sweetheart, we do make a good team. So do Melanie and Owen."

Melanie had returned to the table and sat as far away from the platter of ribs as possible. Owen handed her a bun to nibble and a can of ginger ale. "I wish this kid would figure out morning sickness means morning. Not all day."

Chuckles erupted through the group. Owen

pressed Melanie's head to his chest while her stomach settled.

As soon as Connor loaded his own plate and sat down, Garrett cleared his throat. He moved his attention to his brother when he started speaking.

"Connor, I need to thank you for stepping in and stepping up to lead this family. It's been a rough go of it since we stopped being the Irish Pub Builders with Da. Never thought we'd be together again, but, well, let's just say this is where we belong. MacAteer Brothers Construction and Services helped to save me from a bad place, and I'll be forever grateful to you."

Connor nodded his head in acknowledgement since his mouth was full of coleslaw. He had an inkling where Garrett was headed with this big speech.

Garrett reached into his pocket. "Owen, you and I shared a womb and spent most of our lives next to each other working, eating, drinking, sleeping. So many milestones we've had in our lives together. You found the woman who brings you the peace and the love you've wanted for a long time, and put a ring on her finger. I'm over the moon for you, brother. Maybe we can keep up the tradition of crossing bridges together."

Connor swallowed the bite in his mouth as Garrett presented a box to Bertie.

"I found the ring that is supposed to be on your finger. Will you put it on and never take it off?"

Connor heard Beverly let out a squeak, and she clutched his arm as Garrett offered a single round diamond to his own woman. Bertie took a deep breath as she slipped the ring on her finger. "Melanie? What do you think about double weddings? Want to plan one together?

"Abso-effing-lutely," Melanie stated, her own eyes shining with unshed tears. "But you'll need to find your own honeymoon."

Everyone laughed. Connor's eyes took in the joy on his family's faces.

"No problem there. I'm thinking Ireland. I have a hankering to see where your family started." Bertie let Garrett slip the ring on her finger. The newly engaged couple shared a kiss and Connor looked away as another voice grabbed his attention.

"Bow down, mere mortals. Patrick is in the hooooouse!"

Eva threw back her head. "He's still doing that? Really?"

Connor chuckled as he took a bite of the barbecue. No need to answer his sister. He doubted Patrick would ever stop being his outgoing self. At one time, he found his younger brother an annoying pain in the ass, but Patrick had grown up a lot and found his true place in the world. One that accepted him and that fit him exactly. *Proud of him*, Connor thought.

Patrick walked over with Sloane's hand in his and a cooler in the other. Eva's jaw dropped. "I never thought I see a time when Patrick MacAteer would sucker a woman into being with him."

Sloane shrugged and set up the blender she brought with her. "He saves me a ton on house repairs."

Patrick placed a hand over his chest. "Shot through the heart! I'm dying from a woman's cruelty."

"You are not. Now find me a free plug for the extension cord. I have margaritas to make."

Sloane's remark got more laughs than Patrick's for a change.

Another rumble hit Connor's ear, and he looked up to see his brother Angus and his new lady love, Rhyleigh, pulling up on his motorcycle. They dismounted and approached the picnic table just as Sloane fired up the noisy blender.

"Ooh, I hope you're making raspberry ones." Rhyleigh yelled to be heard above the noise.

"That's the plan."

Melanie raised her cup. "Not for me."

Sloane shook her head as she buzzed the blender. "How the hell did you get pregnant already?"

"Ask Owen."

Patrick stuck his fingers in his ears. "Nope, don't need those details."

Connor almost choked on a bite of food at the easy banter surrounding him. With a smile, he looked at the long tables full of people. At last the entire group was there, sharing food and drink. So many years they had worked and struggled, sometimes together and sometimes divided. They found each other again, in this small mountain city, but now joined with their spouses and future spouses, and their kids and future kids. The happy expressions on their faces meant the world to Connor as he observed the growing clan. True, there were scars from the past. Ones they would carry for a lifetime, but as individuals, they had found the healing force they needed to once again be a family united.

Connor watched the kids as they finished eating and left the table to go shout and play in the grass. Pal and Muttface chased them adding their barks to the kids' screams of delight. His eyes grew wet and his heart filled with a contentment some people could only wish to find. He felt divinely blessed to have it. Connor could only see a brighter and better future in the years ahead as the family grew.

Life is good, he thought as he leaned over to kiss his beautiful wife. She smiled at him and wiped the corner of his mouth with her thumb.

He stood up and lifted his red cup high.

"To the MacAteer family. *Slainte!*"

Enjoyed Rhyleigh and Angus's story? In that case, please consider leaving a review.

If you haven't done so already, check out the complete Dragon Runners MC series, too, starting with the incredible **Mute**.

Looking for a new motorcycle romance to check out? **Doc T**, a sexy motorcycle book in Skye McNeil's Macha MC universe, is now available.

ACKNOWLEDGMENTS

It's been a wild ride writing the stories for the MacAteer Brothers. All five of them are different in personality and experience, but they have the common bond of being devoted to their family and their women.

Angus's story line came up while I wrote Patrick's book. I needed something to set him apart from his older brothers and something that made him distinctive from his twin. A reader joked with me about writing a BDSM book, and I saw a random picture of model tied in an intricate web of ropes, erotic and artistic at the same time. Thus, I started researching shibari and found the perfect secret life for Angus and for Rhyleigh.

I can't thank enough the people that help me along the way during each writing journey. Brittany Alexander for her unbridled opinions, Becky Johnson and her big red pen, beta readers Barbara Hoover, Alicia Woods, Whitney Pogue, and Virginia Gaylor. Your comments and suggestions are spot on and help me see the book through unbiased eyes. Another big thanks goes to all the people at Hot Tree Publishing. Liv, Donna, Lori, Jas, and whoever I missed, I love all y'all for your continued support and your patience in keeping me in line. Last, but certainly not least, I want to thank the readers that have explored the MacAteer family with me. You're the real reason I keep putting the stories in my head on paper.

Slainté!

ABOUT THE AUTHOR

Thanks for reading *Give It To Me.* I do hope you enjoyed Rhyleigh and Angus's story. I appreciate your help in spreading the word, including telling a friend. Before you go, it would mean so much to me if you would take a few minutes to write a review and share how you feel about my story so others may find my work. Reviews really do help readers find books. Please leave a review on your favorite book site.

Don't miss out on New Releases, Exclusive Give-aways and much more!
Join my newsletter: https://www.mlnystrom.com/contact
Visit my website for my current booklist:
https://www.mlnystrom.com/

I'd love to hear from you directly, too. Please feel free to email me at melody @mlnystrom.com or check out my website https://www.mlnystrom.com/ for updates.

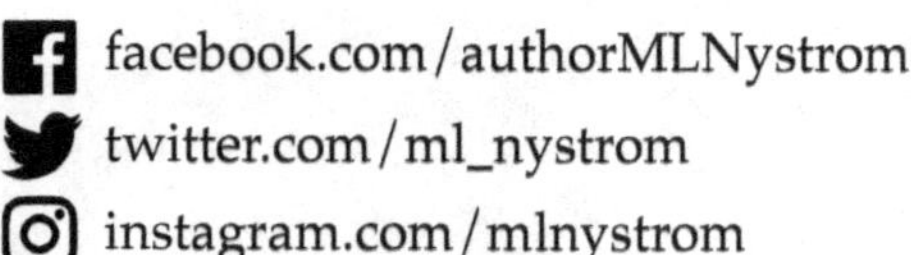

facebook.com/authorMLNystrom
twitter.com/ml_nystrom
instagram.com/mlnystrom

ABOUT THE PUBLISHER

Hot Tree Publishing opened its doors in 2015 with an aspiration to bring quality fiction to the world of readers. With the initial focus on romance and a wide spread of romance subgenres, Hot Tree Publishing has since opened their first imprint, Tangled Tree Publishing, specializing in crime, mystery, suspense, and thriller.

Firmly seated in the industry as a leading editing provider to independent authors and small publishing houses, Hot Tree Publishing is the sister company to Hot Tree Editing, founded in 2012. Having established in-house editing and promotions, plus having a well-respected market presence, Hot Tree Publishing endeavors to be a leader in bringing quality stories to the world of readers.

Interested in discovering more amazing reads brought to you by Hot Tree Publishing? Head over to the website for information:

www.hottreepublishing.com

facebook.com/hottreepublishing
twitter.com/hottreepubs

OTHER BOOKS BY ML NYSTROM

If you loved *Hold It Close*, you might enjoy the other sensual, sexy and romantic stories and books ML Nystrom has published.

DRAGON RUNNERS MC

Mute

Stud

Blue

Table

Brick

MACATEER BROTHERS

Run With It

Ready For It

Hold It Close

Risk It All

Give It To Me

MORE AUTHORS TO CHECK OUT

Looking for more romance across a wide range of genres? Check out Hot Tree Publishing's extensive list.

Amy McClung
    Ann Grech
    Avery Sterling
    Carolyn LaRoche
    Dahlia Donovan
    Eden French
    Eva King
    Gen Ryan
    Genevive Chamblee
    Heidi Renee Mason
    Jas T. Ward
    Jackson Kane

Kolleen Fraser

Krissy V

Laura N. Andrews

Lindsay Detwiler

Mary Billiter

Megan Lowe

ML Nystrom

MV Ellis

Natalina Reis

Samatha Harris

Skye McNeil

Theresa Oliver

Virginia Cantrell